ONE MURDER DOWN

ONE MURDER DOWN

A BEAUFONT SHORT STORY™ BOOK 4

SARAH NOFFKE

MICHAEL ANDERLE

LMBPN Publishing
PMB 196, 2540 South Maryland Pkwy
Las Vegas, NV 89109

Version 1.00, November 2022
eBook ISBN: 979-8-88541-871-3
Print ISBN: 979-8-88541-992-5

THE ONE MURDER DOWN TEAM

Thanks to the JIT Readers

Veronica Stephan-Miller
Diane L. Smith
Dave Hicks
Dorothy Lloyd
Angel LaVey
Deb Mader
Jackey Hankard-Brodie
Christopher Gilliard
Jan Hunnicutt

If I've missed anyone, please let me know!

For Sherlock Holmes.
I know you're still out there. Hiding in the shadows. Solving cases.

MURDER ON A TRAIN

CHAPTER ONE

Adventures rarely start in a safe place that's going nowhere. Most often mysteries can be found where people journey and travel, because those on the move are bound to find thrills.

Paris Beaufont, a fairy godmother in training, had found herself on the hunt for information to solve an important case. That led her to the king of the fae, who then told her that she needed to catch a mystery train to find what she needed.

Things were never straightforward in her world and rarely boring. Paris was almost certain that she'd regret taking on this quest with the flamboyant and ridiculous king, but she had little choice.

Paris had to board a train, not knowing where it was going, but more importantly, with the mission to solve a mystery aboard. That was the only way for her to arrive in the place she needed to find the information she must undoubtedly have.

If she solved the mystery, then the train stopped at the right place. Not solve the mystery and she would find herself perpetually riding the mystery tracks, going nowhere for all of eternity.

Most didn't know that they would have a mystery thrust upon

them. But most didn't live in the strange world of magic, like the halfling in training.

King Rudolf Sweetwater and Paris Beaufont stepped through the shimmering portal to a wide dirt trail surrounded by lush green trees. The air was thick with moisture as if it was about to rain at any moment and the smell of the forest was a stark contrast compared to the city odors where they'd come from in London.

Ahead on the trail was an archway created by a bridge. Directly under it was a small train platform. Paris brushed her blonde hair out of her face and looked around, wondering which way was the train station. It was so quiet in the forest that it felt like they were miles from civilization.

"Where are we?" Paris asked her uncle, the king of the fae.

"In nature," he answered, quite seriously, a pinched expression on his handsome face. "Don't touch anything."

"Why, are there poisonous plants here?"

He pulled a bottle of amber-colored liquor from his coat pocket and eyed it gratefully. "No, I don't think so. It's just that the plants here are so nature-y. Also, it's impossible to regulate the temperature in places like this. Without a moment's notice, water will fall from the sky."

"Do you mean rain?" Paris wondered if she should have brought something to drink too. Maybe King Rudolf would share his cognac with her.

"Yeah, I guess you can call it that," he replied. "Mother Nature really needs to fix things here, if you ask me."

"Again, where are we?" Paris asked.

"Scotland," he replied. "If the locals talk to you, nod and smile. I'm convinced they don't know what they're saying half the time, so how are we expected to."

"I don't think we'll run into anyone here." Paris looked around, only hearing the sounds of birds in the trees and the *whoosh* of wind.

"Oh, I don't know," Rudolf stated. "Someone else might be catching the afternoon train."

"Where do we catch this mystery train?" Paris asked.

He pointed at the seemingly abandoned platform under the archway. "Right there. And we're right on time. The train might be here soon."

Paris glanced down. "There's no train track. And what do you mean, *might?*"

"The Mystery Train shows when it wants," King Rudolf answered. "We better get to the platform. I heard a bird of prey."

"Are they dangerous to us?" Paris wondered if a giant falcon was about to swoop down from the sky.

"No, they signal the Mystery Train arriving." He strode for the platform.

When they'd arrived, King Rudolf sighed, unscrewed the cap from his bottle of Hennessy and took a long drink. Paris glanced both ways down the dirt trail, wondering if she'd wasted her time with this convoluted mission. She needed something important. A piece of information that only a powerful fairy could offer her, and apparently she could only find that person by traveling on this train and solving a mystery.

All she wanted to do was solve her own case as quickly as possible, but doing that hadn't been straightforward. Now she worried that King Rudolf was leading her astray.

"Oh, good, the train will be here in a few seconds." King Rudolf put the cap back on the cognac.

A large buzzard swooped down from the side of the bridge and flew through the archway, gliding low to the trail and flying in the opposite direction. It was quite the mesmerizing sight, but Paris had no idea how that signaled the train.

She glanced back and forth, not seeing signs of the Mystery Train in either direction, although her visibility was quite good both ways. "Are you sure? I don't hear or see a train."

King Rudolf nodded. "Yeah, you wouldn't."

"Right." Paris drew out the word, thinking that either she was losing her mind, or more likely, the fae had.

However, a moment later, to her complete astonishment, a train appeared right in front of them out of nowhere. It was a real train—or appeared to be anyway. Steam issued up from the front of the locomotive. The brakes squeaked as though the train had stopped instead of appearing.

A door to the main cabin opened, inviting them in. King Rudolf held out his arm in a presenting fashion, smiling wide. "All aboard. It's time to take the Mystery Train. Then the games will begin."

Paris gulped, hesitancy in her every move as she climbed onto the train, wondering what this game would be and hoping it didn't get her killed—or make her kill King Rudolf.

CHAPTER TWO

When Paris entered the first cab of the train, the conductor wearing a boxy hat and a uniform greeted her. His black mustache rose when he smiled, transforming his face, making him instantly look younger.

"Welcome aboard the Mystery Train, Paris Beaufont, and King Rudolf Sweetwater." The man bowed.

"You know my name?" Paris pointed at herself.

"Well, of course," the train conductor stated. "I also know that you don't know mine. I'm Peter Peterson."

"Nice to meet you." Paris thought that was a strange name for someone. His parents must have believed it was funny. She looked around at the elegant train cab. It seemed like they entered a time warp and were on a train going across the United States in the 1920s.

"Well, since everyone is aboard now, we'll get going," Peter stated. "I'll go and let our locomotive operator know. Please take your seat. The dining car will be open as soon as we're at full speed."

King Rudolf took a swig from his bottle, indicating a cozy booth. "Good, because I'll be dry in a bit."

Paris sat on one side of the leather booth beside a large window that showed the platform where they'd boarded. Rudolf took the seat opposite her. "So what's this game we're supposed to play and win to find Tiffer, this powerful fairy, who has the information I need to solve my case?"

King Rudolf took another long drink as the train pulled away. Leaning forward, Paris looked out the window, wondering what the scenery would show outside the train.

"It's hard to explain," the fae answered. "All I can tell you is to pay attention to everything you see and hear from this point forward."

Paris watched as the scenery quickly sped by them, showing a blur of green. It was forest and more forest as if they were cruising through the Scottish hillsides, although she figured that magic would be involved and they'd be going somewhere else.

"Okay, I'll pay attention." She peered out the window.

"Not out there." Rudolf stretched to a standing position. "What happens outside the train is irrelevant. You need to pay attention to what's happening *inside* the train."

Paris blinked at him, searching the empty train car. "What do you mean? Nothing is happening in here."

He started for the door on the opposite side, waving at her. "Come on. Papa needs ice for the rest of his Hennessy. Let's go meet some folks."

"You mean there are other passengers on this train?" Paris stood and followed him to the door. "Are you sure?"

He nodded confidently. "I'm certain of it. They're part of the game."

CHAPTER THREE

To Paris' surprise, the dining car was buzzing with people. King Rudolf was correct, and there were other passengers aboard the Mystery Train.

Again, Paris felt that she'd stepped backward in time and was in the 1920s. A very distinguished woman was wearing an elegant blue silk gown with a feather boa collar and fringe on the cuffs. She pulled a long cigarette in a white holder from her mouth at the sight of King Rudolf and Paris and blinked at them as if surprised to see them too.

Gliding her hand over her black curls, the woman extended a hand to King Rudolf as he approached her table, many large rings adorning her fingers. "Well, who do I have the pleasure of making an acquaintance with?" she asked in a dignified voice.

The fae took her hand and kissed the back of it, leaning down low. "I'm none other than King Rudolf Sweetwater, and this is my traveling companion, Miss Paris Beaufont."

"A pleasure." The woman puffed on her long cigarette. "I'm Countess Jessabelle Fairweather. I'd ask you to join me, but I already have an engagement, which should be starting soon now that we're off."

"No worries. We have a table." Rudolf indicated a neighboring table that said, "Reserved for King Rudolf Sweetwater and Miss Paris Beaufont."

"I see you do," the countess said with a pinched smile.

Without another word, King Rudolf sat at the table on the other side of the train car, against the window. Green forest still streaked by outside. Paris glanced around, noticing a waitress on the other end of the car, speaking to a distinguished man in a gray business suit with his black hair slicked back. They appeared to be having a heated conversation, although Paris couldn't hear what they were saying. It was mostly their body language that suggested they were having a disagreement.

Paris didn't hide her interest in the two, remembering what King Rudolf had said about paying attention to what happened inside the train versus outside it. However, a moment later, the gentleman spun and marched toward the countess' table.

As though he might get lost in the narrow car, Countess Jessabelle Fairweather waved in his direction. "Over here, Thomas!"

He pursed his lips and nodded.

Leaning in Paris and Rudolf's direction, the countess said, "That's Thomas Cheetah. He's who I have a meeting with."

"I figured as much." Rudolf held up his bottle to the waitress on the far side of the car. "Can I get some ice, please?"

Catching sight of him, the waitress in a black dress and white apron nodded and disappeared into the next car.

Thomas Cheetah slid into the seat opposite of the countess, sighing slightly.

"What are you drinking, Tom?" She puffed on her cigarette. "I'm buying."

"Oh, Jessabelle, do you really have to play games?" He sounded tired.

"Can't I buy my friend a drink without you thinking I'm up to something?" she asked coyly.

"Are you up to something?" he fired back.

She batted her eyelashes at him in a flirtatious manner. "Oh, Tom, you know that painting will look better in my penthouse apartment. Admit it."

He sighed again, looking out the window. "I knew it. If you wanted the painting, you should have outbid me. That's how art auctions work."

Countess Fairweather blew out a ring of smoke. "You drove up that price past my comfort zone, and you know it."

"Well, may the richer buyer win," Thomas stated smugly. "That's how a free market works."

The waitress returned, carrying two crystal glasses with ice, laying them down in front of Paris and Rudolf, but her attention was squarely on the couple beside them.

"Brittany, my friend and I would like a bottle of your finest cabernet sauvignon," the countess said to the waitress.

"I'll take a whiskey neat," Thomas corrected.

"Oh, do you have to be so difficult?" the countess asked him, irritation heavy on her face.

"Yes," he stated at once.

"Fine, a dry martini for me," Jessabelle said to the waitress.

Brittany turned at once, marching back in the opposite direction, not taking a drink order from Paris or Rudolf.

"Interesting," the fae said to Paris, also watching the exchange and not hiding his eavesdropping.

"What are we supposed to be doing here?" Paris whispered.

He poured the rest of the bottle into the two glasses and slid one over to her. "Watching."

Paris nodded minutely, taking a sip of the Hennessy.

The countess and Thomas Cheetah appeared to be locked in a staring contest when the waitress returned with their drinks. She slid them onto the table in front of the couple and swung around to face Paris and Rudolf.

"Can I get you two anything else?" she asked them.

"Your name, for starters," King Rudolf stated, draining his drink.

"Brittany Jenkins," she replied, putting her hand on her hip.

"I'll take a bottle of cognac," he stated, looking at Paris. "And you?"

She shook her head. "I'm good. Thanks."

"Fine," Brittany said, as if not ordering something was offensive to her. She strode back the way she'd come, nearly running into a man wearing a pinstriped suit and a troubled expression. He had gray hair and a trimmed beard and appeared to be drunk, his glass of whiskey sloshing around as he strode in their direction. It also could have been the movement of the train though, Paris reasoned.

"Hey, good day, chap," the man boomed, setting his glass of whiskey down on Thomas and Jessabelle's table before taking a seat next to them. "I thought I'd find you two here, fighting as usual."

"We're not fighting," Jessabelle fired back, crossing her arms.

"Of course we are," Thomas argued. "It's what we do best."

"I swear, you'd think you two were married, the way you act," the man stated.

"You know I'd never marry," Thomas stated. "A man like me doesn't tie himself to a train track like that."

An audible gasp fell from Brittany's mouth as she dropped a tray on the other side of the train car. Paris looked up, watching as the waitress stooped and picked up the glasses she'd broken.

"It's a bumpy ride today, isn't it, Brit?" the man asked.

She didn't look up but instead rushed out of the car at once, probably embarrassed by her accident.

Rudolf leaned across the aisle dividing them from the other table and held out a hand. "Hello, I'm King Rudolf Sweetwater. And you'd be?" he asked the gentleman.

He offered him a hand, looking as if he might fall out of the seat. "Oh, nice to meet a king. I'm Ronald Whittaker. Yes, I mean, *the* Ronald Whittaker."

The countess sighed and put out her cigarette. "Oh, do you always have to say that when you introduce yourself?"

Ronald waved, fanning away the smoke, nearly knocking over his drink. "Do you always have to blow that smoke on me like that?"

"Which one of these is mine?" Thomas indicated the two side-by-side whiskey glasses.

"How am I supposed to know?" Ronald asked. "Have them both. I'm going to get a nap. Then we'll review those financials, Thomas, old chap."

He stood at once and lumbered in the opposite direction, not paying attention to anything but his path.

The countess and Thomas went back to staring at each other, hostility obvious in their gazes. They didn't look up when Peter Peterson entered from the other side of the train car, smiling with delight.

He halted beside the table and withdrew a cigar from his breast pocket. "Mr. Cheetah, I picked up something recently, thinking of you."

"Is that a Cuban cigar?" Thomas asked, an eager expression on his face.

"Indeed it is," Peter stated. "I know how much you enjoy a fine cigar and thought it might make your journey more enjoyable."

"Why, thank you." Thomas took the cigar, running it under his nose, fondly. "That was very kind of you."

Brandishing a silver lighter, Peter created a flame, holding it out for Thomas. "Think nothing of it, Mr. Cheetah."

The other gentleman's eyes flicked up, an edge of stress in them as he puffed on the cigar, getting it lit. He blew out a puff of smoke and nodded at the train conductor, seeming to dismiss him. Without another word, Peter strode back the way he'd come.

"A nice man, he is," the countess said.

"Yeah, I guess." Thomas sipped from one of the two glasses of whiskey in front of him.

"Oh, you don't like anyone, do you," Jessabelle stated tersely.

"What's there to like?" Thomas puffed on his cigar and swirled the whiskey in his glass.

"Really, you're infuriating. I could strangle you," the countess said, standing at once and marching out of the car, not having taken a single drink of her martini.

Thomas laughed humorlessly, shaking his head. He looked about to take another drink when his eyes bulged, and the cigar fell from his hand. He then dropped the glass, making it clatter onto the table in front of him, and fell to the side, stiff as a board, toppling to the floor—dead.

King Rudolf clapped as if this had all been a show. "Now it begins."

"What begins?" Paris asked, her eyes wide with shock as she stared at the dead man before them, lying on the carpet of the train charging along.

"Our game," King Rudolf stated victoriously. "There's been a muuuurder! It's our job to solve it."

CHAPTER FOUR

"Solve it?" Paris ran her gaze over the man stretched out beside them. "That's the game? To solve the murder? Does that mean that Thomas Cheetah isn't really dead?"

"Oh, he is, and it sounds like he deserved it and was loathed by many, which will make our jobs more difficult, by design," Rudolf stated. "To get off this train, we have to figure out who done it and exactly how and why. Only then will the Mystery Train stop and we'll find Tiffer."

"What a strange game." Paris wasn't as repulsed by the sight of the dead body as she thought. "Is it always a murder mystery that has to be solved to find Tiffer?"

Rudolf nodded, leaning down to inspect the body.

Paris picked up a napkin from their table and used it to pick up the still smoking cigar, afraid that it was about to start a fire. She blotted out the ash on the carpet and put the cigar in a tray on Thomas and Jessabelle's dining table. "So when you said that you couldn't explain the game because it was complicated, you couldn't simply say, there will be a murder, and we have to solve it?"

Leaning his head to the side, the king of the fae studied

Thomas. "If I told you that, you would have been on edge. Most don't react well when they know someone is about to be murdered. I told you to pay attention, and I hope you did. They presented us with everything we need to solve this murder."

She studied the two glasses of whiskey on the table beside Jessabelle's untouched martini. "So much happened at once. It seems that everyone hated Thomas. I'm no coroner. How do we know what the cause of death is?"

"We don't." Rudolf stood. "There are forensic spells we can do, but they'll take time to lead us to the cause of death. Even then, we have to know who did it and, more importantly, why."

"What if we don't figure that out?" Paris watched the green scenery continue to streak by the train window outside.

"Then we won't get off the Mystery Train." Rudolf rhythmically flicked his hands. Paris guessed he was performing the forensic spell to find information on the cause of death. "One time, I spent the better part of a year on this train. That was my first time trying to locate Tiffer and pretty much the reason I put a hit on her."

Paris nodded, gulping down the tension in her throat. "I can kind of understand why you wanted to kill her now."

He chuckled. "I was alone then and didn't have your keen eyes to help. Oh, and I was sober, which we both know isn't when I think best."

"I hope it doesn't take us long to solve this murder." Paris looked around the dining car for any clues. "I really need to find this fairy and get the information to solve my own case."

"You will," Rudolf stated with confidence as the train doors on either side of the car slid back. Having been alerted by the fae yelling, "There's been a murder!" the others had come running. From one end, Peter Peterson and Ronald Whittaker entered, halting in shock at the sight of the dead man on the floor. On the other side of the car, Brittany Jenkins and Countess Jessabelle

Fairweather entered, also stopping at once. The waitress covered her mouth as a scream ripped from her lips.

Rudolf glanced at Paris. "While we wait for forensics to come back, the most important work of our detective case begins. It's our job to question these suspects." He looked back and forth between the two men and the two women on either side of the car—shock heavy on their faces. "One of these people here is our murderer, and it's our job to find out who it is and why they wanted Thomas Cheetah dead."

CHAPTER FIVE

"I didn't kill him." Countess Jessabelle Fairweather strode back and forth in the open train car, another long cigarette in a white holder in her shaking hand.

Not wanting to disturb the corpse and also not wanting to stare at a dead man's body, Paris and Rudolf had moved the interviews to a neighboring train car. This one was open with chairs against either side of the windows where the scenery hadn't changed outside still.

"That's exactly what the murderer would say." King Rudolf sat casually in one of the seats, his legs crossed as he watched the countess' frantic movements.

Paris sat beside him, taking in all the nonverbal cues from the first suspect they were questioning. They'd sequestered the others to the first car where they were sitting in silence when Paris and Rudolf had left them.

"I'm not a murderer," Countess Fairweather argued, offense heavy on her face as she continued to stomp back and forth, her black high heels leaving small impressions in the plush carpet as she walked.

"That's for us to decide." Rudolf picked up his fresh glass of cognac.

"How did you know the victim?" Paris asked.

"We were friends," Jessabelle answered at once, blowing out a plume of smoke.

"Friends?" Rudolf argued, arching a discerning eyebrow at the woman. "When we saw you in the train car, you and Thomas Cheetah were arguing, were you not?"

Halting, Jessabelle threw her hands up. "Well, yes, but…"

"I believe the last thing you said to Thomas was, 'I want to strangle you," Paris remarked, remembering the scene vividly.

"That's right." Rudolf nodded at her. "If that doesn't sound like a threat of murder, I don't know what does."

Countess Fairweather gawked at them, laughing. "Oh, come on. That's an expression. I didn't want Thomas dead. I wouldn't dirty my hands on that man's neck."

"So you're not upset that he's dead, then?" King Rudolf questioned. "Because if you're friends, well, I'd be sad if one of my friends died."

"Of course I'm upset," the countess argued. "I'm in shock, can't you see? Thomas was always trying to get under my skin. He was an infuriating man, but I didn't want him dead."

"What were you two arguing about right before he died?" Paris asked.

"Oh, that was nothing." The countess waved dismissively.

"We'll be the judge of that," Rudolf stated with confidence.

She sighed dramatically. "Thomas and I are both art collectors. I have an extensive collection, and I'm always on the hunt for a prized piece to add. Recently, Thomas and I were at an art auction, and he kept driving up the bid for a painting."

The countess' lips pinched together, and heat flared on her face. "He didn't want that piece. I know it. The painting was Rococo, and I know with certainty that Thomas didn't like that style of art. He outbid me to make me crazy."

"Why would he do that?" Paris questioned.

"That was what Thomas did," she answered. "He wasn't happy unless he was cheating someone or taking something that belonged to them. He was an awful man."

"Also not a way that I would describe a friend." Rudolf took a drink.

"Fine, we weren't friends," the countess admitted. "We competed for the best art. We ran in the same circles. We often found ourselves in the same places."

"So, as the old phrase goes, you kept your friends close and Thomas, your enemy closer," King Rudolf observed.

A disingenuous smile flicked to Jessabelle's mouth. "You know all too well as a king that powerful people can't afford not to keep an eye on their enemies. If I took my eye off Thomas, that's when he'd swoop in and steal the best art pieces."

"It sounds like he had, outbidding you at the auction," Paris suggested. "What were you trying to get Thomas to do when you were arguing?"

"Give me the painting, of course," she answered. "He didn't want it. I was willing to trade one of my statues for it. I know how Thomas loves his Roman statues, all clogging up his family's estate."

"If you wanted the painting so badly, why didn't you outbid Thomas?" Rudolf asked.

Hesitation flickered in the countess' large brown eyes. "The Fairweathers have fallen on hard times. Our empire isn't as wealthy as it once was and Thomas knew that."

"So you couldn't afford to outbid him, then," Rudolf guessed.

Jessabelle shook her head, her black curls falling over the side of her face, covering up the shame. "That stubborn man knew it, and he didn't want the painting. He didn't want me to have it."

"So you killed him for revenge!" Rudolf exclaimed victoriously.

She gasped, covering her mouth. "Of course I didn't. I would never resort to such things. Who you need to be questioning is Ronald Whittaker."

"Why?" Paris noticed the glint of mischief rise in Jessabelle's eyes.

"He was Thomas' business partner," she answered. "If anyone could have benefited from his death, it would be Ronald."

"How did you know the victim?" Paris sat across the train car from Ronald Whittaker, the second suspect for them to question.

Unlike the countess, Ronald seemed much more at ease, lounging back in a chair, his tan loafer resting on his knee. "That old chap and I've been business partners for the last year."

"Business partners?" Rudolf questioned, standing and striding back and forth in the train car much as Jessabelle had done. However, his demeanor was scrutinizing as he worked out the clues.

"We'd started a company together," Ronald answered. "A real estate venture. We both had a fifty percent stake in the investment, and it was doing quite well thanks to my genius decision making."

King Rudolf glanced at Paris with a calculating expression. She thought she knew what he was thinking right then. However, he could as easily be deciding that he wanted a peanut butter sandwich. It was hard to tell with the fae.

"With Thomas dead, the company will now be one hundred percent yours?" Paris guessed.

Ronald nodded. "Naturally. That was the agreement we had set up."

"So you benefit from Thomas' death," King Rudolf accused, pointing at Ronald, who didn't appear flustered.

"Oh, I bet that's what Countess Fairweather said, didn't she?" he asked, annoyance on his face. "You can't believe a thing that woman says." He laughed rudely. "Fairweather is the perfect name for her because when she wants something, she'll be all nice to you. As soon as she gets what she wants, she'll cut your throat and not think twice about it."

What Ronald was saying didn't sound far off from the truth, Paris thought. Jessabelle had admitted to keeping her friends close and her enemies closer. It seemed that she was using Thomas.

"What motive would the countess have for killing Thomas?" Paris asked. "They didn't appear to like each other very much, but that seems to be common rivalry."

Another chuckle popped out of Ronald's mouth. He still seemed inebriated from earlier. "People kill others for a lot less than a common rivalry, but that's putting it mildly. The countess hated Thomas Cheetah. He was always outbidding her at art auctions, knowing that she couldn't pay the high prices he could. I mean, despite some of his faulty decisions, our company was starting to rake in the dough. However, Thomas' considerable family inheritance gave him a rather large spending budget for silly artwork."

Ronald shook his head. "I mean, really. Two seemingly reasonable people wasting their money on art. It's absurd."

"Do you think the countess murdered Thomas out of anger and tired of being humiliated at auctions and losing to him?" Rudolf speculated.

"No, chap, I don't," Ronald answered at once. "I think she murdered him for that frilly Rococo painting she was obsessed with."

"Yes, but Thomas won the bid at auction," Paris countered.

He narrowed his judgmental eyes at her. "Oh, have you never been to an art auction and don't know how it works?"

"Shockingly, I haven't spent much time hobnobbing with snobs at art auctions," Paris said dryly, not sure if she disliked Ronald or Jessabelle more.

"Yes, you don't seem the type." Ronald ran his snooty gaze over Paris, obvious disapproval in his expression. "If you were familiar with how art auctions work, you'd know that if something happens to the top bidder before they finalize the paperwork, the prized artwork goes to the runner up."

"So Countess Fairweather will now get the painting," Rudolf guessed, striding back and forth again, excitement in his voice.

"Exactly, chap," Ronald stated. "Thomas was poisoned. Who was sitting with him and had access to his drink?"

"We're not sure how he was murdered yet," Paris stated.

"You laid your drink down next to Thomas'." Rudolf halted, narrowing his eyes at the man before him. "You could have switched the drinks. They were both whiskeys."

Ronald laughed as if this was the most ridiculous thing he'd ever heard. "Thomas might make many questionable decisions, but he knew how to drink right. We both preferred whiskey as our drink of choice."

Paris tilted her head speculatively. "You didn't much care for Thomas, did you?"

"I think you'll find that no one liked the man," Ronald answered matter-of-factly. "Many referred to him as Thomas Cheater because he'd do whatever it took to win, profit or get the upper hand."

"Then why would you go into business with such a man?" Rudolf questioned.

"Simple," Ronald chirped. "Thomas was loaded. Our business required capital."

"And you didn't have enough money to fund it on your own," Paris guessed.

"So you switched your drink with Thomas', thereby poisoning him," Rudolf speculated, combing his hand over his chin. "Now, with him out of the picture, the company is all yours."

"I'd had a drink from that whiskey before I entered the train car," Ronald argued. "I had quite a bit to drink and left to take a nap."

"But you didn't take a nap," Paris observed. "Why is that?"

"Because I ran into Peter Peterson and he was trying to sell me on a new business venture," Ronald explained. "Now that's a man with a good head on his shoulders. He'd make good business choices, basing the decision on reason rather than greed. Alas, I had to turn the chap down."

"Why is that?" Rudolf questioned.

"Well, he doesn't have the capital," Ronald answered. "He has the ideas and the drive, but I'd be funding the whole thing. Poor guy works nonstop to make ends meet. When his parents passed, they didn't leave him a single dime. I mean, they gave him that awful name, Peter Peterson, then they died and gave all their fortune to their younger son.

"According to Peter, his brother is a real ingrate, squandering the family fortune. Anyway, unfortunately, I had to turn Peter down. A real shame too. I'd like to work with him. Not a single time I haven't seen him smiling. He knows customer service, treating all of us with such kindness."

Paris nodded, having remembered seeing Peter Peterson present the Cuban cigar to Thomas, knowing he enjoyed such things.

"You didn't much like Thomas as your business partner, did you?" she asked, having picked up on several cues that suggested this.

"Is it that obvious?" Ronald laughed. "He was always making illogical decisions. If he didn't have deep pockets, I would have never gone into business with him. I planned to buy him out once things took off."

"Or kill him and take the company," Rudolf accused, picking up his tumbler and taking a drink.

Ronald gritted his teeth. "I didn't kill Thomas."

"You did want the company all to yourself, didn't you?" Rudolf questioned, and Paris quietly had to commend his style of questioning.

"Of course. But murder? Come on now," Ronald argued. "I know it appears I have a motive to kill him, but I wouldn't risk something like that for money. You know who would, though? Someone motivated by love or rather a scorned heart."

"Someone was in love with Thomas?" Rudolf questioned.

Paris' eyes widened with a sudden realization. "Brittany Jenkins, the waitress. She and Thomas were together?"

Ronald laughed. "She wished. No, he was using her, but the broad fell for his act. Now, if someone wanted to kill him, it would be the woman who he dumped."

Apparently too upset by seeing Thomas Cheetah's dead body, Brittany Jenkins needed time to compose herself before being questioned. After consoling her with a hug, Peter Peterson agreed to interview next—joining Paris and Rudolf in their interrogation train car.

"How long have you known the victim?" Rudolf asked the train conductor, having resumed his seat.

"Oh, for quite some time." Peter looked much more regretful about the death than the other two they'd questioned. "He was often on the train, going here or there for business meetings."

"So you knew him well, then?" Paris asked.

"I don't think anyone really knew the man who was Thomas Cheetah, to be honest." Peter shook his head. "He wasn't the type of person who showed people who he truly was."

"You knew he enjoyed Cuban cigars?" Rudolf questioned.

"I make it a habit to know what my customers enjoy," Peter said, a proud smile on his face.

As Ronald Whittaker had said, Peter seemed like a genuinely nice person.

"Did you see anything suspicious before Thomas' murder?"

She thought the train conductor was in an ideal position to see the various behaviors of the suspects.

"I can't say that I did," he admitted. "Ronald had too much whiskey, but that's typical on these legs of the trip. He's a happy drunk, and rarely do I have any problems with him."

"You were with Ronald when the murder happened," Rudolf stated.

"I was," he answered.

"What were you discussing?" Paris tried to corroborate the various stories.

"Well, he'd mentioned the countess and Thomas were fighting again," he replied. "I knew the two would be at it for most of the trip. Jessabelle was only on the train to try and convince Thomas to let her have the painting she'd lost out to him at auction."

"Is that right?" Rudolf leaned back in his seat with a glint in his eyes.

"It's true," Peter Peterson answered. "Honestly, it was the only reason that Ronald was on the train today too. They both wanted something from Thomas, and getting time with him is never easy. He's a very busy man, always riding the rail between his estate and his various meetings."

"This estate, where is it?" Rudolf questioned.

"On the outskirts of London," Peter answered. "The train goes right by it on every route. Thomas had his very own private platform installed there so he could get between there and his meetings more easily."

"Quite the man of show, exerting his wealth like that," Rudolf stated. "You'd think he owned the train."

"He practically did," Peter stated. "Without his business, well, I'm afraid I'd be out of a job. We'd have to minimize our use of the train significantly. Most days, Thomas is our only customer, but he pays us handsomely to use the Mystery Train."

Paris offered him a sensitive look. "Now that Thomas is gone, what will happen to you? To the train?"

Peter sighed, looking off. "I'm afraid I'll have to look for another job. Now they'll cut my hours so drastically that it won't be enough to support me."

"I'm sorry," she offered thoughtfully.

"Did you and Ronald Whittaker discuss anything else before the murder?" Rudolf leaned forward.

Peter thought for a moment. "No, I believe that was it. He was going to take a nap and grab some financials for Thomas before dinner when we heard you exclaim that Thomas was dead. That's when we ran through the train to the dining car."

"Right." Rudolf drew out the word, giving Paris a pointed look. They were both curious about why Peter didn't disclose that he pitched a business idea to Ronald right before the murder. Or maybe it was the businessman who was lying about the train conductor wanting to go into business with him. Still, the questions were: who was lying and why?

"You said that Ronald was on the train to see Thomas as well, right?" Paris asked. "Why was that?"

"Oh, he wanted to buy him out of their business," Peter answered. "I don't think he could take dealing with Thomas one more day. They were constantly butting heads on the train about various business decisions. The whiskey made for volatile conversations between them. Although Ronald was usually a happy drunk, Thomas was known for getting quite belligerent."

"Interesting." Now it was Paris' turn to draw out the word. There was another inconsistency. Ronald had said he was waiting to buy Thomas out once the business had taken off—not that he was planning on negotiating it that day. Something wasn't right there.

"Were you aware that Thomas and Brittany Jenkins were in a relationship?" Rudolf asked the train conductor.

He nodded, looking suddenly more somber. "Yes, and that had been another source of conflict on the train. Brittany idolized Thomas, having fallen for his charm and money. She would always get distracted as we neared his estate, about to pick him up from his private station."

"Having the fancy estate on display from the train was a way to flash his wealth around," Paris observed.

"I think so too," Peter said. "But Thomas was done with Brittany, having lost interest in her. He'd told her that she was a simpleton and they never had a future."

"Ouch." Rudolf hissed as if burned.

Peter nodded. "It was rather heartless, but that's how Mr. Cheetah was, and Brittany knew that. She thought she could change him, but I think that was very shortsighted of her."

"You can't change the soulless," Rudolf offered.

"Brittany would have fixed the drinks that she served to Thomas and the countess, correct?" Paris asked.

"Well, yes," Peter answered. Then his eyes widened with alarm. "But it wasn't Brittany. She'd never harm Thomas. She'd never harm anyone. She might have been heartbroken, but she isn't a murderer."

"People do crazy things when they're hurt," Rudolf stated.

"Not Brittany," Peter argued. "She's the sweetest woman. So very loving and kind."

"Well, if she's ready, we'd like to question her now." Paris rose to her feet.

Peter stood too, heading for the door. "I'll go and fetch her, but please be sensitive with your questions. She's still very shaken, and I know that she's not the murderer."

CHAPTER EIGHT

As Peter had said, Brittany was still distraught when she entered the train car for questioning. Her face was puffy and red from crying, and she had a monogrammed handkerchief clutched in her hand, which she used to wipe her tears often.

"I'm sorry for your loss," Paris said, realizing that Brittany was probably the only one sad that Thomas Cheetah was dead.

The waitress opened her mouth to say something, but only a croak came out before she burst into more tears.

"Did you poison the victim?" Rudolf asked in a mad rush.

Paris spun to face her partner with an offended look. "Remember the request to be sensitive. Brittany is very upset."

"I'd be upset too if I'd killed someone," Rudolf spat. "I mean, so far, she has the best act."

Brittany blew her nose on the handkerchief, shaking her head. "It's not an act. I wouldn't harm Thomas. I'm devastated that this has happened to him."

"Are you more devastated that he's dead or that he dumped you?" Rudolf asked.

Paris wanted to slap the fae, but she reasoned that they were playing good cop, bad cop at this point.

"It's true that Thomas had broken things off with me," Brittany said through more tears, "but I have to admit that I saw it coming. I didn't think I ever had a future with him. He was a rich businessman, and I'm only a lowly waitress."

"Money doesn't matter," Paris urged. "Who someone is deep inside is what counts, and Thomas sounded like a real jerk— taking advantage of everyone."

"I know, but I wanted to believe that at his core, he was a good person," Brittany argued.

"You wanted to change him." Rudolf drained his drink and shook the glass. "Is it too much to ask that you get me a refill?"

"Yes," Paris answered at once. "We're conducting an investigation."

"Fine." Rudolf sighed. "You fixed the drinks that you served to the countess and Thomas before he died, correct?"

"Well, yes, but…was Thomas poisoned?" Brittany asked.

"We'll ask the questions," Rudolf fired back, appearing to be having fun with the questioning all of a sudden. Or maybe it was a crying woman who was bringing out a different side of him. He didn't appear as at ease as with the others they questioned.

"The bottle that I poured from was freshly opened. I broke the wax seal myself," Brittany explained. "Countess Jessabelle had given it to Thomas when she'd come on board."

"The bottle of whiskey was from her?" Paris asked, this getting her attention.

"She knew it was Thomas' favorite. It was a twenty-year-old whiskey, and she had given it to him when they boarded," Brittany answered. "He'd then handed it to me for the bar."

"The countess originally ordered a bottle of red wine for the two of them," Rudolf mused.

"I didn't understand that," Brittany stated. "Countess Fairweather never drinks wine, but maybe she was hoping that it would soften Thomas up. That's why she'd given him the whiskey, hoping he'd cave and give her the painting they were fighting about."

"She'd given him the whiskey, and instead of keeping it, he gave it to you for the bar." Paris tried to work out the details. "The glass of whiskey you poured for Ronald, was that from the same bottle?"

"Oh no." Brittany shook her head. "That was Thomas' whiskey, and I wasn't pouring that for anyone else. I poured Ronald's from a bottle that was already open."

"Interesting." Rudolf stroked his fingers over his chin.

"Peter says that you were often distracted when the train neared Thomas' house," Paris began. "Were you worried about how things would be when you weren't together, and he was on the train?"

"Well, of course." Brittany wiped her nose with the handkerchief. Paris noticed the initials were T.P. "But I didn't kill him. I was going to quit after today. I couldn't bear going by Thomas' estate every day or seeing him on the train. Now it won't matter. Without his business, we'll all be out of a job."

"That handkerchief." Paris pointed at the linen cloth Brittany was holding. "Whose initials are those?"

Brittany glanced at the embroidery as though she hadn't noticed it before and blinked in surprise. "Oh, I must still have Thomas' handkerchief. He gave it to me when he broke things off when he first got on the train today. I broke into tears, obviously upset, and he gave me this, telling me not to overreact and make a scene."

"I think the real mystery is how no one murdered Thomas Cheetah sooner," Rudolf remarked, shaking his head.

"Yes, Thomas Cheetah," Paris said, drawing out the names. "So his initials would have been T.C., not T.P., right?"

Brittany shook her head. "Cheetah wasn't his real name. Few knew that, but I discovered it when I'd seen the guest list one time. Peter had left it out, and only legal names are listed there."

"So what's Thomas' legal name?" Rudolf asked.

Brittany's eyes diverted. "I'm not sure I can say. No one knows. Peter doesn't know that I figured it out or that I saw the guest list by accident. I asked Thomas about it at one point, and he told me the truth."

"Someone on this train murdered a man," Paris urged. "If you can give us any information that can help, you need to explain what you know. Otherwise, it won't look good for you."

Brittany had trouble swallowing for a moment. "Well, I don't see what help it can be to your investigation. It's only some family secrets. You see, Thomas went by the surname Cheetah, but his real name was Peterson. No one except the two of them, Thomas and Peter, knew that they were estranged brothers."

CHAPTER NINE

"Things just got a lot more interesting," King Rudolf said as he and Paris reentered the murder scene.

Thomas Cheetah's body, or rather Thomas Peterson's, was still sprawled out where they'd left it. It was more than curious to Paris that Thomas and Peter were brothers and the train conductor hadn't mentioned it. However, when putting together all the clues, there were a lot of curious pieces of information.

No one seemed innocent of committing the murder. Strangely, everyone had a motive, a means, and something that tied them to the actual event.

King Rudolf held out his hand, and a moment later, a Sherlock Holmes-type pipe appeared in it. He held it up to his mouth and pretended to take a puff, one of his eyes squinting as she pictured the famous detective doing when contemplating an investigation.

"So let's review the facts," King Rudolf stated. "I spent a lot of extra time on this train before because I threw out solutions to the crime. I think to make our time more concise, we are smarter to think things through and come up with one murderer, the motive, and the means."

Paris nodded. "So if we throw out conjecture, we'll be penalized. That makes sense."

King Rudolf chewed on the end of his pipe. "Tiffer is an insufferable woman who knows her power is in great demand and makes those who want it work for it."

Paris leaned over the table where Thomas Cheetah and the countess had drinks. She picked up one of the glasses of whiskey and sniffed, then the other, not sure what she smelled for, but thinking that if one held poison, she might pick up on it.

"So Brittany Jenkins prepared all the drinks," Paris began. "Which means…"

"She would have the perfect opportunity to poison the one served to Thomas," King Rudolf stated.

"Or the poison could have come from the bottle of whiskey that Countess Jessabelle Fairweather gave to Thomas upon entering the train," Paris imparted, holding up a cautionary finger.

"True," the fae chirped. "The poison also could be in Ronald Whittaker's glass, and maybe he added it before entering the dining car."

"The forensics spell will be done soon, right?" Paris asked.

He nodded. "That only tells us how Thomas died, not why or by who. So we have to work out what we know and that hopefully was revealed in the interviews."

"Countess Jessabelle Fairweather had a reason to want Thomas dead," Paris stated.

"Oh, for sure," Rudolf affirmed. "With him out of the picture, she'd own the art auctions. She came on the train today specifically to meet with him."

"Ronald Whittaker also had a reason to get rid of Thomas," Paris argued.

"And he or Peter Peterson lied about their conversation during the murder," Rudolf agreed. "Ronald said that Peter proposed a business deal, but the train conductor didn't mention that. So what would be the reason to say that to us or omit it?"

"Well, and Ronald didn't tell us about how the two were talking about Thomas and the countess fighting," Paris remarked. "Why omit that?"

"Of course, Peter left out the bit about him and Thomas being brothers," Rudolf pointed out. "But if that was my brother, I don't think I'd want anyone to know either."

"Yes, and apparently Ronald knew that Peter had a brother, but it doesn't sound as if he'd connected it," Paris mused. "He also was caught lying because he told us that he was going to buy Thomas out at some point. Peter said he was on the train today to negotiate that with him."

"The scorned lover has the most reason for murder," Rudolf stated. "I mean, people do things for money, power, and love. But murder, well, that's almost always a crime of passion."

Paris and the fae king were quiet for a long moment, both of them lost in thought as they studied the murder scene. There was a lot of information to consider. Also, there were a few pieces of glaring information that kept rising to the surface in Paris' mind.

She thought she could work out what had happened, but it wasn't the logical progression of events based on the facts. It was taking a few leaps of faith, and Paris knew they needed something more concrete.

As if the universe was trying to help her out, something sparkled around the dead man's body.

King Rudolf rubbed his hands together excitedly. "Oh, the forensic spell is about to reveal how Thomas died. If it was poison, it will glow where it found evidence."

A second later, three places glowed bright orange.

Paris searched the scene, taking special note of the details. Then she looked up at King Rudolf. "I think I know who done it."

He nodded. "Yes, me too. Are you ready to go and convict our murderer?"

Paris grinned, looking at the passing green scenery outside the train, hoping they would soon get off it.

CHAPTER TEN

All the suspects and Paris and King Rudolf gathered in the train car where the interviews had taken place.

As before, Countess Jessabelle Fairweather was striding the length of the car, smoking her long cigarette in its white holder. Ronald Whittaker was lounging in one of the armchairs, looking over his nails as if he didn't have a care in the world. Peter Peterson was anxiously looking between the guests as though concerned about their wellbeing. Brittany Jenkins had busied herself serving a round of drinks to all those in the train car.

Paris took the cognac she was handed with a polite smile. "Thank you for gathering here for what we believe will be the reveal and resolution to this murder mystery. We know that it's been a very stressful evening for everyone."

"Stressful doesn't begin to describe it." Countess Jessabelle Fairweather took the martini that Brittany handed her and sipped it. "One of you is a murderer, and I'm stuck on a train with you."

"Well, you say that as if you're not the criminal at large." Ronald sipped his whiskey.

The countess clapped her hand to her chest. "Me? I'm not capable of such things."

"You very much are." King Rudolf stood, his hands clasped behind his back as he revolved on the room of suspects. "What's important to remember is that each one of you was capable of murdering Thomas Cheetah. Not only that, but you all had the means, the motive, and the opportunity. But only one of you committed the crime."

"Well, it wasn't me," Countess Jessabelle Fairweather said in a shrill voice. "I hated Thomas. I'll be the first to admit it, but I wasn't about to go to jail to take him down. He probably hoped I would. Then he'd get the last laugh."

"You did give him the bottle of whiskey though, as a faux gift." Paris narrowed her eyes at the woman.

"I was trying to endear him to me so he'd give me the painting," Jessabelle stated.

"An open bottle of whiskey," King Rudolf added, throwing a scrutinizing gaze at the countess.

"It wasn't open," she nearly exclaimed, pointing at Brittany. "Ask her. She'll tell you it was sealed."

"It was. I opened it myself." Brittany nodded furiously.

"It appeared to be unopened," King Rudolf corrected. "When my partner and I investigated the bar, we discovered that someone broke the seal on that bottle long ago."

"I didn't poison Thomas!" the countess exclaimed.

"No, you did what you thought was worse," Paris remarked. "You knew that Thomas was a snob when it came to fine whiskey, but he really couldn't tell the difference. So you brought him the bottle of twenty-year-old whiskey, making him think that you were giving him something of great value.

"However, you filled that old bottle with bad whiskey and worked hard to reseal the bottle or at least make it look resealed. A waitress who hardly ever opened an old bottle of whiskey such as that on a train wouldn't know the difference because Brittany thought that if a wax seal covered the cap, then it had to be unopened."

"I smelled the whiskey you gave Thomas," Rudolf continued. "What you had in the bottle was the cheap stuff. If you couldn't beat Thomas at his own game, you were going to give him bad whiskey, hopefully a headache the next day, and humiliate him by telling everyone he drank bad liquor and couldn't tell the difference."

"Maybe that's all true." The countess thrust her nose up haughtily. "But I didn't kill Thomas."

"It's all true," Paris said with confidence. "And no, you didn't."

"Are you certain?" Ronald Whittaker asked. "My money was definitely on the greedy countess."

"Speaking of greed," King Rudolf said in a booming voice. "You, Ronald, had boarded the train with the intent of getting Thomas drunk, hoping to convince him to sell his shares of the company to you."

"I did not," Ronald argued. "I told you that I was waiting until the company was doing better."

"A smart businessman such as yourself would know that Thomas would never sell once the company was doing well," Paris stated. "No, the best time to sell would be when things looked bleak, and it would be most advantageous to Thomas to get out. So you decided that you'd get him drunk by leaving behind your glass of whiskey, knowing that he couldn't leave a good drink to go to waste."

"Well, that hardly proves anything," Ronald retorted, then sipped his drink and shook his head.

"You're right," Rudolf stated. "Which was why we searched your room for the financials you said you'd be reviewing with Thomas over dinner."

"How dare you," Ronald seethed in an offended tone.

"We dared," Rudolf snapped. "What we found was quite inter-esting. The financials appeared to be doctored, telling a tale of a company not doing so well. A smart businessman such as Thomas Cheetah, under the influence of whiskey, would have taken one look at those and decided to bail out of the company."

"Well, the company wasn't doing very well," Ronald stated.

Paris held up a finger, pausing him. "You told us that despite Thomas' bad decision-making, the company was. Your story isn't adding up, Mr. Whittaker."

"I did want the company," Ronald boomed. "Thomas was going to run it into the ground. What did he care if it did well? He had his family money. So what, that I was willing to lie and cheat to get my share of the company? I deserved it. But I didn't kill him."

"You did lie and cheat," Rudolf said victoriously. "But you're correct. You're not the murderer."

Paris and Rudolf both turned their scrutinizing gaze on the waitress and train conductor in the corner. They had both gone silent and white, not making a single noise.

"I didn't want him to die," Brittany wailed, nearly breaking into tears again.

"No, you didn't," Paris consoled. "You loved Thomas very much. You wanted him to marry you, but when he refused, you lost it, storming off and making quite the emotional scene."

"I was upset," Brittany explained. "How else was I supposed to react? He'd broken my heart."

"So you killed him," Ronald accused.

"Of course not!" Tears streamed down Brittany's face.

"No, it wasn't Thomas you wanted dead," King Rudolf stated. "You told yourself that he'd love you. That if he could see you for who you are, that you'd be enough. You thought someone else was the problem—flaunting her fancy ways in front of Thomas."

"No, no, no!" Brittany said in a rush, shaking her head frantically.

"What?" Peter stepped forward, looking between the detectives and the waitress. "What is going on?"

"Brittany didn't try to kill Thomas," Paris explained. "She did love him. Because of that, she believed the reason he'd broken things off with her was because of Countess Jessabelle Fairweather." She pointed in the other woman's direction, making her eyes pop open with alarm.

The countess pressed her hand to her chest. "Me? And Thomas? Oh, how absurd. I couldn't stand that man."

"No, you couldn't," Paris continued. "But what Brittany witnessed as your disdain for each other, she interpreted as lust."

Jessabelle laughed loudly, a ring of smoke popping out of her mouth. "That's so irrational."

"It might be, but it still was enough for murder," King Rudolf stated.

"I didn't murder Thomas!" Brittany yelled.

"No, you didn't," King Rudolf continued, looking the waitress over. "But you did try to murder the countess, didn't you?"

Brittany's bottom lip quivered. Her hands knit together. She looked close to bursting. Then she nodded. "Yes, yes I did."

"What?" Countess Jessabelle Fairweather nearly yelled. "You witch!"

"I thought you were the reason Thomas dumped me." Fresh tears rolled down Brittany's cheeks.

"He dumped you because you're a poor waitress and he was a bitter old man," the countess fired.

"You won't speak to her that way!" Peter cut in.

King Rudolf stepped between the feud, holding up a hand to pause them. "Now, thankfully for the countess, she was so consumed with making Thomas look like an idiot by drinking bad whiskey that she didn't take a single sip of her martini. If she had, it would also be her murder that we were solving because Brittany poisoned it."

"You tried to murder me!" the countess yelled, looking close to jumping across the train car and strangling Brittany Jenkins.

However, Paris also stepped forward, serving as a barrier to the brewing fight. "She didn't, and that's not the murder we're solving. Only one man died today, and we know exactly who did it, how, and why."

In unison, Paris and King Rudolf turned to face Peter Peterson, disappointed expressions of conviction on their faces.

"Me?" Peter Peterson pressed a hand to his chest. "I rather liked Thomas. I think I was the only one who liked him for who he was."

"That's because you were the only one who *knew* who he really was, but even then, you couldn't let go of past grievances." King Rudolf started to pace, his hands still behind his back. "You see, Thomas was your best customer and treated you very well, giving you lots of business."

"Then why would I want to kill him?" Peter argued, throwing his hands up.

"Because as Thomas did all things to minimize people, the best way to humiliate you would be to make you depend on him for business," Paris continued. "So he created the private train station outside his house, making it appear that he was going to be the Mystery Train's bread and butter. However, he conducted most of his business in London according to the financial records we found in Ronald's room, which was close to his estate."

"There was no reason for Thomas to take the Mystery Train on a regular basis," King Rudolf added.

"He took it for meetings," Peter stated.

"He took it so he could flaunt his business and wealth in your face," Paris boldly corrected. "He did it so you had to pass his estate every single day and see exactly what you didn't have."

"What is she talking about?" Ronald Whittaker scratched under his beard.

"Peter Peterson is the older of two sons," King Rudolf began.

"I know that," Ronald cut in. "Peter told me that his younger brother was insufferable and that their parents gave him the family fortune. That's why he asked if I'd go into business with him." Ronald gave the train conductor an apologetic look. "I'm sorry, old chap. It's not for me."

"Peter did make that proposal right before Thomas' murder because he knew that he was going to need a new job," Paris continued. "Because he knew that his very best customer was about to die."

"You knew!" Brittany spun to face Peter.

He lowered his chin, his eyes searching the carpet as if that's where he could find answers to this mystery. "No, I didn't know. I wanted a better opportunity. A new life. A way to take care of myself."

"You knew that Thomas was about to be murdered," King Rudolf countered. "Because you're the one who gave him the poisoned cigar."

Gasps echoed all around the train car.

"It was the cigar?" the countess asked in shock.

Paris nodded. "Forensics showed poison in three places at the murder scene." She held up a finger. "The first was the martini glass, which we all know that Brittany put the poison into the countess' drink."

Jessabelle glared at the waitress, looking ready to murder her.

"There were also remnants of poison on Thomas' mouth," Paris continued. "They were a direct match to the cigar which he'd been smoking moments prior and received as a gift from you, Peter Peterson."

"Why would I want to murder my best customer?" Peter yelled, his voice irate and his face flushed red.

"Because he wasn't only your best customer," King Rudolf said triumphantly. "Thomas Cheetah was many things to you, but the least important was a client. He was the guy who'd stolen the girl you were in love with."

Brittany gasped, covering her mouth, looking between Rudolf and Peter.

"He was your estranged brother," Paris went on, earning more shocked sounds from those in the train car.

"And he was the man your parents gave their entire fortune to, having always favored him," King Rudolf concluded.

"Thomas Cheetah, also known as Thomas Peterson, was the brother who didn't win gracefully," Paris explained to the captive audience of wide-eyed people in the train car. "He stole his parents' favor, convinced them to give him their fortune, and flaunted it in Peter's face every single day."

"Peter knew that showing his animosity was what his younger brother wanted," King Rudolf stated. "So he refused and served with a smile. But soon, he couldn't take it anymore. Thomas had everything that Peter wanted. So the older brother decided that he'd steal Thomas' business partner, create a rift with Brittany to break them up, pin the murder on the countess who had every motive and means to kill Thomas, then committed the crime. Unfortunately, Peter Peterson, all the evidence pointed to you."

Paris gave the train conductor a long look full of shame and remorse. "You, Peter Peterson, are the one who murdered Thomas Cheetah."

As she finished her conclusion, the brakes of the Mystery Train screeched, and for the first time since they boarded, it came to a grinding halt, bringing them to their destination.

Paris Beaufont had solved the mystery and she'd be delivered to the powerful fairy—and one step closer to solving her own case.

Life was a wild ride and full of one mystery after the next.

MURDER AT A MANSION

CHAPTER ONE

Front Step, Glenbogle Manor, Scottish Highlands, Scotland

Paris Beaufont, whose day job was more of a ring master for secret agents, had to find Sherlock Holmes.

Many thought the great detective was fictional. Some, who knew that wasn't true, thought he was dead. But Paris' sources had told her that he was simply in hiding. And she needed his and only his expertise to crack a very important case.

The hard part was drawing him out of hiding. According to Sherlock's old assistant, Dr. John Watson, that involved creating a murder mystery that the great detective simply couldn't resist: a murder mystery. Sherlock Holmes apparently had a radar for unsolved mysteries.

He always showed up for them, even if the authorities didn't know it. And he didn't leave until he had solved the case for his own curiosity, even if no one knew the truth he uncovered.

Paris, with the help of her uncle, the king of the fae, had set the scene for a very real murder to take place. They had picked Ramy Vance to be the victim. You see, this man had fallen into the fountain of youth and therefore couldn't die—not easily, anyway. This made him the perfect target for a murder mystery.

And although liked, many had grievances with Ramy, making him a likely victim. He was often killed by his friends, knowing that in an hour, he'd return, smiling and fumbling around, making a mess for others to clean up once more.

Hopefully during the weekend, Ramy would be murdered. But since he was immortal, so to speak, his death wouldn't be a real loss. But it would be a murder and who had done it, a mystery that only Sherlock Holmes could solve—drawing the great detective out of hiding. Then Paris could offer him a job that hopefully he couldn't resist. The man apparently loved a challenge, and she had her fair share of those to offer. There was one particular mystery that only Sherlock Holmes could solve, so she was going to do everything possible to bring him out of hiding.

Firstly, Paris and King Rudolf had to set the scene for this murder to take place. That involved putting the right people together, under the right circumstances. Then they should be able to sit back and watch as people bickered, sabotaged and hopefully killed someone.

The first guest made their way down the gravel driveway, which *crunched* under their vehicle's tires. It was time for Glenbogle Manor's weekend guests to arrive.

"Are you sure that one of these people will commit the murder?" Paris asked King Rudolf, suddenly feeling overly nervous. Maybe it was the pressure to draw Sherlock Holmes out of hiding. Perhaps it was because they had to have a murder for that to be a possibility. Or maybe it was that she had to spend the weekend with some crazy and dangerous people.

Most likely it was a mixture of all three.

"Don't worry your pretty little head, lassie," Rudolf chimed in a bad Scottish accent, his hands clasped behind his back. He'd dressed elegantly in a white shirt, bow tie, and jacket with a green and blue tartan kilt. The king of the fae even wore the traditional sporran, kilt hose, matching tartan flashes, and ghillie brogues.

"I've ensured that all the guests have a grievance with Ramy, our would-be victim, which isn't a hard thing to do. Furthermore, they all know that he can't die—"

"Easily," Paris interjected, feeling underdressed next to the king in her usual leather jacket and all-black outfit. Still, she had her wand and potion belt, prepared for whatever adventure happened, whereas Rudolf looked ready for a traditional ceilidh dance party.

"Right, Ramy Vance can't die easily," Rudolf amended. "However, all the guests know this and will have the opportunity, means, and motive to commit a murder, knowing that it won't count since he's seemingly immortal."

"These people are sort of my friends," Paris argued. "I don't want to think that they'd commit murder. Are you sure?"

Rudolf gave her a look that said, "Oh, you poor naïve soul," and smiled. "Most people will kill Ramy without issue. However, the invitations I sent out said that this weekend was about settling scores. If an argument needs to happen, so be it. If a punishment, then let it. All guests have been encouraged to let out their emotions. But please, pray for me."

"You?" Paris questioned. "We've made it so the guests hate Ramy."

Rudolf nodded. "Yes, but one of them is arriving now, and it's my darling wife, Serena, and she's cross with me with a full invitation to let her emotions out."

"What did you do?" Paris asked dryly.

"I was born, Paris. I was simply born…"

CHAPTER TWO

Front Step, Glenbogle Manor, Scottish Highlands, Scotland

Queen Serena Sweetwater arrived at the large estate driving a shiny red Cadillac DeVille convertible. Her long brown curls flew behind her as she sped down the driveway, sending rocks into the air and throwing up dust.

Paris had met Serena, but she'd spent little time with the mortal who'd married the very eccentric Rudolf Sweetwater. Their love story was right out of the fantasy books. Well, if those books were about an evil queen who killed Serena in cold blood so she and Rudolf couldn't be together. Then the fae, not yet king, risked his life and Liv Beaufont's to bring Serena back to life—taking years off his time but receiving the crown of the fae in return.

Although Serena was a mortal, married to a fae who would live a thousand years or so, special magic granted her a long life like her husband and three halfling children. The Captains, as the triplets were known, were the only other halflings in the world besides Paris. However, they were half-mortal and half-fae, not as powerful a combination as being magician, fairy, and a little demon.

The Captains' names were classic Rudolf. He named his three daughters after his heroes: Captain Morgan, Captain Silver, and Captain Kirk. The very high-maintenance girls took after their mother in that they were insufferable. Still, they'd inherited their father's intelligence, which meant it was best if they didn't interact with the public.

The brakes made an awful screeching noise as Serena abruptly halted the car. The woman exuded the confidence one would expect from King Rudolf's wife as she checked her face covered by oversized sunglasses in the rearview mirror. There was little reason for sunglasses since it was overcast. It wasn't a day in the soggy Highlands to have the top of the convertible down either, but that didn't seem to matter to Serena. Maybe it was because she was on vacation. However, Paris thought the mortal's life was one big vacation.

Serena stepped out of the car as Rudolf opened the door, dressed in a leopard print pantsuit with a black scarf tied around her neck and wearing impossibly high heels that were bright red. She leaned over as Rudolf welcomed her, allowing him to kiss her cheek.

"So happy you could make it, dear." Rudolf winced as though afraid she might slap him from the start.

"My bags and the dog are in the back." She didn't glance at her husband, her eyes on Paris. Her voice was deep and reminded Paris of the iconic Mae West. "Fetch them, doll face."

"Of course, my love," Rudolf sang, shutting the door and digging into the back.

Serena strode over, her stiletto heels precariously wobbling in the gravel. She held up the keys to the convertible, swinging them in front of Paris' face. "If you want a tip, don't get any dust on my baby."

"You think I'm the valet?" Paris pointed at herself.

"Of course you are, dressed like that." Serena lowered her

sunglasses and looked her up and down. Her voice sounded so much like Mae West that Paris half-expected her to say, "Why don't you come up some time and see me."

Rudolf jerked his head up suddenly. "Oh, honey, that's my niece, remember? Paris."

"You mean, Liv's child?" Serena pulled her glasses off her face and looked Paris over now. "She doesn't look dead. Are you sure she is? If she is dead, I want her secret. I looked a right mess when I was deceased."

"Oh, good, this is pretty much how this weekend will go," Paris muttered mostly to herself.

Rudolf hurried over, carrying two large suitcases and a little Yorkshire terrier under one arm. "No, dear. I said that Paris went away while her parents were missing. Remember, I told you that she was back now that the danger hunting her was gone."

"Honestly, you expect me to listen all the time." Serena reached out and took the dog, nuzzling the animal. "The dog and I really can't be expected to have such pressures on us."

"Are you going to name that thing?" Rudolf indicated the animal with a red bow and probably a pedigree to beat Paris'.

"I told you, I want to name him Captain Silver so you have to tell our daughter that she's giving up her name," Serena stated.

"She's an adult," Rudolf argued. "We can't rename her now, especially to give her name to the dog."

"Of course, we can. I say we name her Sailor Sweetwater."

"She's taking a demotion?" Rudolf threw his hands up but forgot he had heavy suitcases in them, the movement a bit ungraceful.

"Have the conversation with Sailor, then the dog gets her name, and everyone is happy."

"I don't think Captain Silver will be very happy about giving her name to the dog," Rudolf imparted.

"Where is my room?" Serena turned her attention to the large manor. "I need a drink and a nap, or someone is getting murdered."

Rudolf hurried up the stairs with the bag. "No murders yet, dear. What did I say? Not until after everyone gets here."

CHAPTER THREE

Front Step, Glenbogle Manor, Scottish Highlands, Scotland

Ahead of Paris a few yards away, a portal opened, shimmering bright blue. Paris squinted from the light but saw the expert potions maker step through from the streets of London to the highlands of Scotland.

Bep, the owner of the Rose Apothecary potions shop in London, wore a long black traveling cloak and a disappointed expression as she took in the large manor. "I heard that I won an all-inclusive trip to Disney World. Is that Epcot Center?"

Paris glanced at the huge mansion and shook her head. "No, that's round, and this is a house in Scotland. You did portal here, remember?"

Bep waved her off, closing the portal. "How can I? That was so long ago."

"Riiiiiight. Well, thanks for joining us. We thought it would be nice to have your company during the weekend." Also, Paris knew that Bep despised Ramy, so she was a natural choice.

"I don't want anyone to talk to me," Bep said at once. "I'll be reading my books, enjoying peace and quiet, and expecting all my meals delivered to my room."

"We have dinner in the formal dining room," Paris corrected. This would only work if she forced people to spend time together and therefore get on each other's nerves and kill Ramy.

"Fine, I'll have dinner with the others, but that's it."

"Also, we have a few activities planned for the weekend, and all supervised by experts. I think you'll enjoy them…"

Bep narrowed her eyes at Paris, pulling down the hood of her cloak and fluffing her short curls. "I don't enjoy things. I tolerate them. I allow you all to interact with me. But I never have and will never be the one having a jolly time during a weekend at the Magic Castle." She pointed at Glenbogle at Paris' back.

"That's a house, and again, this isn't Disney World."

"Fine, you settled for Disneyland." Bep sighed. "I'll put it in my Yelp review."

"I don't have a Yelp…I'm not running a business." Paris glanced around. "Do you have any bags?"

"No, I planned for you to provide all my clothes and toiletries this weekend."

"Too bad I didn't plan for that. I'm sure we can round up some wellies and other things for your journey through the moors."

"I expect so." Bep picked up the hem of her cloak and marched up the stairs into the manor.

Paris sighed, turning her attention to welcome the next guest. To her shock, he was already standing squarely in front of her, although a head or two below her gaze.

CHAPTER FOUR

Front Step, Glenbogle Manor, Scottish Highlands, Scotland

Paris flinched back, putting a few inches between her and Quiet. The gnome with a flat expression and red nose wore his usual work clothes, dressed warmly for his chores in the mountains.

Quiet was the groundskeeper for the Gullington—the headquarters for the Dragon Elite. It was just up the road from where they were in Scotland, although Paris had never been there since only dragonriders could enter.

However, she'd met Quiet when she opened Little Pleasures farm-to-table restaurant in Colorado. Sophia, Paris' aunt, had recruited Quiet to help with setting up the farm and grounds. When things were running smoothly, the gnome and expert in landscape management had turned over the responsibilities at Little Pleasures to Paris' boyfriend, Hemingway.

Paris hadn't seen the mysterious gnome since he'd left Colorado to return to his job at the Gullington. However, Paris knew that while he was at Little Pleasures, tending to the crops, he'd lost an entire season of roses in the garden due to Ramy Vance. The guy who had trouble following him around accidentally brought an infestation of bugs with him on a visit, and they took out most of the plants that bloomed.

It took Quiet months to rid the property of the infestation. Also, the extermination project required Quiet to spend extra time at the farm, taking him away from the Gullington longer than he'd planned. Paris was pretty sure that the extra work and time spent away from the Gullington would make the gnome want to murder Ramy if given a chance.

He would get it…as well as a gun.

Paris and Rudolf weren't leaving anything to chance. They were going to ensure that whiskey flowed like water all weekend, tempers were high, and many weapons were accessible.

Never before did Paris think that she'd be working so hard to encourage murder. But when they caught Sherlock Holmes, it would all be worth it. Except for Ramy, who they were painting as everyone's enemy in hopes that someone killed him.

"Hey, Quiet." Paris smiled down at the little gnome.

He didn't return the grin, but he did nod.

The nickname Quiet wasn't a coincidence. Not only was the groundskeeper for the Dragon Elite soft-spoken, but he seldom said anything.

"Thanks for joining us and agreeing to take the group on a hunt," Paris stated. She wasn't a big fan of hunting parties, but desperate times called for desperate actions. Also, Paris knew enough about this group to know that most couldn't shoot a grouse to save their life. She hoped they tried to shoot Ramy, not worried about his life.

Quiet nodded again and moved around Paris, striding into the manor.

Of all the guests for the weekend, the silent gnome might be her favorite. However, something materialized through the gray sky, and Paris realized that a surprise pair of guests were arriving —and they took the prize for her favorites.

CHAPTER FIVE

Front Step, Glenbogle Manor, Scottish Highlands, Scotland

"Sophia! Lunis! You made it!" Paris exclaimed, running over to greet the blue dragon and his rider when they landed on the green lawn in front of the manor.

"Of course we did." Sophia slid off her dragon and hurried over to hug Paris. "You're throwing a party down the street from the Castle. How can we not make it?"

"I'm throwing a murder. It's not really a party," Paris corrected, her voice low. She'd told Sophia about the situation when she looked for a manor to rent for the weekend. Also, she'd asked Sophia's permission to borrow Quiet for the weekend.

"Have you been to one of Sophia's parties?" Lunis folded his blue wings and grinned at Paris. "They feel like murder."

Sophia flashed her giant dragon a threatening look. "Watch yourself, or it will be you this weekend and not Ramy."

"Oh, you and your threats," the blue dragon scoffed. "That's fine because I plan to live forever. Or die trying..."

Sophia let out a long breath, glancing at her niece. "If jokes could kill, Lunis would be your murderer."

"I don't see why everyone is so uptight when it comes to

death," Lunis continued like he hadn't heard Sophia. "It's life's way of saying 'slow down.'"

Sophia gave Paris a commiserating look. "Are you sure you want us here for the weekend? The dragon won't stop with the jokes. It's like a curse."

"You must stay for the weekend. I think we'll have a great time," Paris insisted and winked at the dragon. "You know what, I was wondering about something, Lunis."

"What's that, halfling?"

"What happens when you get scared half to death twice?" Paris hid her grin.

"Oh, nice one!" Lunis laughed.

Sophia shook her head, turned, and marched for the house. "I think it's going to be a long weekend."

"Hey, Soph!" Lunis called after her. "Did you hear about my friend who got crushed by a piano? His funeral was very low-key…"

CHAPTER SIX

Music Room, Glenbogle Manor, Scottish Highlands, Scotland

Almost everyone had arrived at the estate for that weekend's event. One person was fashionably late. He must have known that for him, this was going to be a deadly affair.

Sitting around the music room, Paris watched as Bep took a drink from the waiter handing out champagne. Serena was lying across the chaise longue, looking like she'd already polished off a bottle of wine with her head back, an arm over her closed eyes, and her dog perched beside her.

Sophia was pecking the keys on the piano, making a nice melody. With his neck through the large open picture window, Lunis had his head bobbing around the space, spying on every-one. Quiet sat in the corner, polishing an old revolver as he studied the room.

"May I have everyone's attention?" Rudolf *clinked* something against his glass to make a dinging sound. "Although I hoped to make our first cheers of the weekend when everyone was here, I think I'll go ahead and do it now."

"Who else is coming?" Serena asked, peeling her arm off her face and blinking around, probably seeing stars.

"Oh, nobody," Rudolf replied dismissively. "But if you don't like it when people are late, just remember that this person disregarded the time on the invitation."

Paris rolled her eyes at the king of the fae, who wasn't subtle.

"I, for one, love it when people are late to my parties." Bep downed her drink and motioned for the waiter to bring her another. "The best kind of party I could throw would be one where no one showed up."

"I don't think you understand how parties work," Serena stated judgmentally.

"In fact, I do, child," Bep countered. "But I love the idea of hosting a party, cleaning up the house, making lots of food, and no one showing up. Then I have a perfectly wonderful place to enjoy my treats and no one to ruin it."

"You're very strange." Lunis shook his head at her.

"You're an oversized lizard with wings, but I've decided that I'm tolerating you for the weekend," Bep sounded dignified before she swallowed the next flute of champagne in one go.

"I've decided not to eat you this weekend," Lunis offered, turning his attention to Sophia playing the piano and humming slightly. "Play us a song. Just don't make it country."

"You don't like country music?" Rudolf sat in a large chair next to Paris.

"I don't," Lunis replied. "I mean, I don't mean to denigrate those who do." The blue dragon looked around the large room full of people and musical instruments. "For those of you who like country music, denigrate means to 'put down.'"

"Oh, that joke was bad…" Sophia shook her head and played louder.

Rudolf and Paris laughed. Bep shook her head in disapproval. Quiet muttered something inaudible.

Serena sat up. "I don't get it."

"Don't worry. There will be more that you might get," Lunis promised.

"You know, I was dreading this weekend." Bep made the waiter give her the bottle of champagne so she could refill her glass on her own.

"Thanks," Paris muttered dryly.

"I mean, you all aren't really my type of people," Bep continued, not hearing Paris. "You talk too much, too loudly, and are generally unpleasant to be around."

"I sense that a compliment is on the way," Paris whispered to Rudolf.

"No doubt." He nodded.

"However, although I'd rather be eating saltine crackers and watching my cats bat something around on the kitchen floor," Bep continued.

"Oh, who wouldn't?" Lunis chimed in.

"I'm glad to be here with you all." Bep smiled around at the group and held her glass up.

"Me too," Serena cheered, picking up a bottle of champagne that Rudolf had left for her and holding it in the air. "You all aren't as bad as I remembered."

"Thanks." Sophia played still louder.

Quiet picked up a glass of whiskey sitting next to him and held it in the air, muttering something the others couldn't hear over the piano music or probably without it.

"Well, then cheers," Rudolf sang, holding his glass high. "To fun with friends."

"Cheers!" Paris called with the others as they all *clinked* the nearest glass and drank, most emptying their drink.

The butler entered at precisely that moment, opening the double doors to the music room, his chin low. "The last guest has arrived. May I present Mr. Ramy Vance."

He stepped aside to reveal the shorter man with a duffle bag slung over his shoulder and a carefree, goofy grin. "Hey ya, guys!" Ramy waved rather ungracefully.

"Oh, dear, kill me now," Bep groaned, refilling her glass.

"Don't kill me," Serena complained. "Kill that guy." She pointed at Ramy standing in the doorway.

Quiet slung back his drink, wiping his mouth with the back of his hand as he bitterly mumbled something that sounded like, "I'd like to do the honors."

Paris glanced at Rudolf, who nodded victoriously. They might have set the perfect stage for murder.

CHAPTER SEVEN

Music Room, Glenbogle Manor, Scottish Highlands, Scotland

Paris knew why everyone at the estate hated Ramy and wanted him dead…well, as dead as possible. If anything, people wanted to act on their anger because they knew the special little man couldn't really die. All of the motives for death were ones of passion.

Quiet despised Ramy because his careless act with the bugs had cost him months of work and taken him away from his home for longer than necessary. The gnome was a chill little guy unless something took him away from his most righteous responsibility of caring for the Dragon Elite.

The groundskeeper might be a very ethical person, but if given the opportunity and knowing that the consequences wouldn't be lasting, he'd take his chance to make the annoying Ramy Vance pay for his actions.

Bep's grievance was purely about money—one of the biggest things connected to passion. Most in London knew that the success of Heals Pills was due to the incredible products they sold, which had so many wonderful healing properties. However, the loyal customers raved up and down the lane about the store clerk they adored.

Even when Bep made an elixir that competed with what they sold at Heals Pills, she couldn't compete with his customer service. More times than she cared to count, the potions expert had lost sales to Ramy Vance, whose klutzy nature seemed to endear him to people rather than push them away.

Bep remained convinced that if she did away with the store clerk, her store, the Rose Apothecary, would gain on the competition. Or at least, she'd feel marginally better for the solid hour that Ramy was dead. She could at least tell the customers that she killed him and stood over his dead body, making her feel better the next time he stole a sale from her.

Serena Sweetwater loathed Ramy out of the biggest, most dangerous of all passions—love.

For years, Rudolf had been late from work because he was at Heals Pills working on inventory or doing marketing. Often he admitted it was because Ramy messed something up that he had to fix. In her delusional style, Serena had interpreted this to mean that Ramy was moving in on her territory.

She knew better than to say something to her husband. Instead, she quietly harbored bitterness toward Ramy Vance, believing he was the reason she got less affection at the end of the day.

Serena was jealous of the time the store clerk spent with Rudolf. She would never say anything. She didn't think her husband was the unfaithful type. Still, she believed that Ramy stole Rudolf's time and energy. If given the opportunity, she was going to take her revenge.

It didn't matter that killing him wouldn't last. It would make her feel better. The next time Rudolf came home late, she'd smile and remember how she tripped Ramy off a cliff and watched him fall to his death.

Paris glanced around the room of would-be killers wondering

which one would strike first, satisfying their need to make Ramy pay. She didn't know, and that was for the best. It was up to the great detective to discover "who done it."

Now she and Rudolf had to sit back and wait, let Ramy get murdered, and catch Sherlock Holmes when he showed up to solve the murder. If they'd done their job, this would be such a complex case that the great detective wouldn't be able to resist.

CHAPTER EIGHT

Music Room, Glenbogle Manor, Scottish Highlands, Scotland

It had been over an hour since Paris had heard from Faraday. She realized that she was overly worrying. The squirrel was probably busy investigating at Fairyland Studios. However, he'd promised to check in with her "every hour, on the hour."

It wasn't like Faraday to go back on his word. It did seem a little overly protective of Paris to require him to check in so much. She reasoned that when she'd made him promise, it was more a figure of speech and she'd hear from Faraday as soon as he was free or had something to report.

The piano music was soon drowned out by people yelling. First, Serena told Ramy off for always hogging all her husband's attention. Then Rudolf was screaming because he thought she called him a pig. Then Bep joined in, saying that all the businesses that sold potions on Roya Lane should close except hers.

In the corner, Quiet swayed back and forth, drinking straight from the bottle of whiskey. Paris glanced at her Aunt Sophia, who smiled in return. They both knew that everything was going as well as it could. Setting people up to kill one particular person was no easy work. However, things were heated. Most wanted Ramy dead and there were plenty of opportunities to do it.

Paris stood and clapped to get everyone's attention. "How about we all get ready for dinner?"

"Why don't you mind your own business," Bep scolded and tottered out of the room, holding an empty champagne bottle. "I'm not hungry for dinner. I'll take wine in my bedroom and a bubble bath."

"That makes two of us." Serena stormed for the exit too.

Bep turned, shaking her head and the empty bottle at the mortal. "Oh no. I don't bathe with other people."

Serena backed up in horror, waving in front of her. "No, I didn't mean that I wanted to bathe with you...I simply meant... well, I don't have to explain myself. Out of my way, woman. I'm going to run a bath."

"I'm going to get more wine," Bep slurred, turning and swaggering out of the music room.

Quiet got up, carrying the revolver he'd been polishing, and hobbled for the exit too.

"Quiet, will you be joining us for dinner?" Paris asked hopefully.

The gnome turned, shook his head, and pointed the gun up. Paris braced herself, wondering if he was going to shoot it. He did, but it only *clicked* loudly. The gnome blew on the barrel and holstered it before turning and striding out and down the corridor.

Ramy grinned nervously, looking all around. "Well, it looks like a fun group you've put together. A bit of a mixed crowd that I wouldn't have paired, but I'm sure we'll have fun. What are the plans for tomorrow?"

"A funeral," Rudolf said, seemingly lost in thought.

"A fun time," Paris said in a rush. "What my uncle meant was a fun...time. Fun for all. Especially you."

"Me?" Ramy asked, blushing. "Why me?"

"Well, because so many love you so much," Lunis stated, his neck still snaked through the open window, which was starting to chill into the room. "They just aren't here."

"How about more music?" Sophia tried to cover for Rudolf and Lunis, the same as Paris.

"Yeah, that sounds nice," Paris stated in a rush.

Lunis shook his head. "I don't know. I'm still a bit nervous about music."

"Why is that?" Ramy asked.

"Well, because I woke up last night to find the ghost of Gloria Gaynor standing at the foot of my bed." Lunis pretended to shiver like the chill of the air, or the fright of his story had gotten to him.

"Oh, no." Ramy shook his head with fright too. "That sounds scary."

Lunis nodded. "Yeah, at first I was afraid...then I was petrified..."

"Please stop or I'll murder you," Sophia stated dryly, playing a long deep note on the piano, making an ominous sound.

"That's fine," Lunis chirped. "I'm not afraid to die. I just don't want to be there when it happens..."

No one laughed, which only encouraged the blue dragon. He huffed, blowing smoke from his nostrils, and shook his head. "Really, though. I've been thinking about buying a burial plot. It's just that I feel like it's the last thing I need."

Again the room remained silent like they were at a wake and trying to show respect to the dead.

Lunis smirked, glancing at Paris. "I'm thinking of getting buried in a glass coffin."

"Oh, yeah?" She decided to play along.

"Who knows if they'll be successful. Remains to be seen."

At the punch line to this joke, Sophia played another deep, long note on the piano. "And now, I think I've lost my appetite and the will to live."

"Hearing you talk like that makes me angry." Lunis shook his head. "You know what else makes my blood boil?"

"What?" Paris encouraged the blue dragon.

"Crematoriums!" Lunis chuckled loudly. Paris did too.

The rest of the group simply exchanged annoyed looks.

"Okay, but in all seriousness, I'm not sleeping out here like some commoner," Lunis complained. "Where are my quarters?"

Rudolf strode for the exit to the music room. "I've got a nice place for you and Sophia in the basement. It's a bit dark and dank, but there's an easy way to get down there, and it's cozy."

"Dark, dank, and cozy," Lunis droned, shaking his head. "Don't list places on Airbnb. Oh, and I'm going to need the Wi-Fi password."

"There isn't one," Rudolf explained.

Lunis nearly screamed, which seemed strange coming from a prehistoric dragon. "Are you insane? You know you need to password-protect your Wi-Fi, right?"

"No, there isn't any Wi-Fi," Rudolf clarified.

Lunis glanced at Sophia. "Here I thought you were taking me on vacation this weekend. Now I realize you were taking me to hell!"

"Don't worry, Lun," Paris offered. "I can get you Wi-Fi using a hack the squirrel taught me." She held up her phone, suddenly remembering that bad reception wasn't why Faraday hadn't messaged her—having consoled herself with that idea earlier. It simply had to be that Faraday was busy working the case. She needed to make him proud by working on her own case. He'd be so happy when he met the real Sherlock Holmes.

"Oh good, one of you isn't a savages," Lunis stated. "I'll come around to the basement."

"You can come through the dining room if you want to grab dinner first," Rudolf offered.

"I'm starving." Ramy rubbed his stomach. "I'm so hungry that I feel like it could kill me."

"Don't let it," Paris warned, suddenly serious. "Just wait for someone to stab you in the back before you die."

He gave her an uncertain look and nodded. "Sure…that must be one of your weird fairy games. Maybe we can play later. All I know for sure is that I'm craving some mushroom broth, a cup of cold thistle tea, and a hard bed."

Ramy strode out of the music room and for the dining room at once. Lunis, Sophia, Paris, and Rudolf all looked at each other in bewilderment.

Finally, the blue dragon said, "Seriously, what's wrong with that guy? Who craves mushroom broth?"

"Or cold thistle tea?" Paris asked. "Isn't that a weed?"

Sophia nodded. "And who wants a hard bed?"

Rudolf shrugged. "I don't know, but if someone else doesn't kill him, I might."

CHAPTER NINE

Dining Room, Glenbogle Manor, Scottish Highlands, Scotland

Paris was starting to lose hope…she thought that plotting to get someone to kill Ramy wasn't going to work. Serena had taken to her room with the dog and told Rudolf to leave her alone for eternity or the rest of the weekend, depending on which lasted longer. Bep had come down to dinner, but only to move around champagne bottles, splashing liquid all over the table when they fell. Quiet was simply sitting in the entryway of the manor, once again polishing the revolver he'd brought.

Paris, Sophia, Rudolf, and Lunis had supper with Ramy, making small talk and trying not to act nervous. However, if this didn't work, Paris didn't know how they'd lure Sherlock Holmes out of hiding. The thought that she might fail at this brought a whole host of concerns to her mind.

No matter how much she tried, she couldn't shake her worry about Faraday. She tried not to check her phone too often but found excuse after excuse to look at her screen.

"Well, I for one, can't wait to shoot some dogs tomorrow during the hunt." Rudolf yawned and stood when dinner was over.

Sophia shook her head, standing as well. "You take dogs on the hunt. You don't shoot them."

"Well, I'll shoot, and you use that." Rudolf pointed at Inexorabilis on Sophia's hip. It was her mother, Guinevere's sword—the woman Paris was named for. The sword, which was elfin made and beautiful in every regard, was one of Sophia's pride and joys. The sight of it gave Paris a thought.

"Hey, Aunt Sophia, can I talk to you?"

"Of course." Sophia patted Lunis on the side of his face. "Go brush your teeth, and I'll tuck you in."

"Hah-ha. I'm going to raid the pantry for cookies." Lunis withdrew his head from the dining room and lumbered around toward the kitchen.

"Well, I'm off to bed." Ramy waved at the group.

"Goodnight." Paris waved.

"See you in hell," Rudolf offered, waving too.

"What did you say?" Ramy was suddenly serious.

Rudolf shook his head. "Nothing. My wife told me to leave her alone, so I'll go to my room. It's like every night at my house."

"Yeah, I think I might need something to sleep." Ramy took his goblet of wine that he'd left undrunk since he'd focused all his attention on his mushroom broth and cold tea. He took a long sip, downing the wine before shaking his head. "Well, I'm ready for that hard bed."

"Right." Paris smiled. "See you tomorrow."

"See you," Sophia said.

The pair watched as Ramy left, leaving them alone. Then Paris turned, asking her burning question to her aunt.

CHAPTER TEN

Front Step, Glenbogle Manor, Scottish Highlands, Scotland

The night hadn't been a total loss, Paris thought as she sat on the front steps of the estate, cold but enjoying the night air. She and her aunt had sat out there talking about bonding to weapons. Sophia had shared how she bonded to her sword—Inexorabilis. Her aunt then explained that any good weapon was something you relied on but remembered that you couldn't be overly dependent upon it.

That's when Sophia claimed that carrying her sword all night had been more than clunky and excused herself to bring it to the basement where she'd be sleeping with Lunis. She returned and further explained that based on what Paris shared with her, she might have bonded to Amantis, or wand, or maybe it would take more acts of faith.

Each weapon was different and had unique qualifications. Paris would know when and if she bonded to Amantis. Then she'd have new advantages. The fact that Amantis had already showed her where to find information on the love meter and Watson was cool enough for her. She couldn't wait to find out what advantages she had later.

Paris was about to quiz her aunt more on weapons and bonding with them when there was a loud commotion inside the house. It sounded like something fell, clattering and breaking on the floor. This was followed by Rudolf yelling, 'Oops, that was me. My bad." Then there was a loud *bang*.

Paris and Sophia exchanged confused looks and broke into laughter. One never knew what King Rudolf would do—either pull off an impressive acrobatic move or fall on his face. The odds were usually fifty-fifty.

Since Sophia was always busy with the Dragon Elite and Rogue Riders and Paris was always preoccupied with her life, they rarely found time together just for them. So Paris treasured the opportunity to spend an extra bit of time with her aunt on the manor's stoop, staring out at the dark grounds. She appreciated Sophia's thoughtful advice. She loved that Sophia was a good listener, hearing her concerns about Faraday. Then she loved it more when the dragonrider kissed her cheek and told her to get some rest and that everything would look better in the morning.

That was before a scream, running footsteps, and tons more commotion sounded inside.

Then several servants ran out and exclaimed in unison, "Ramy Vance is dead!"

Paris knew that she should be remorseful, but she couldn't be happier. She didn't know how, why, or who, which was exactly as she and Rudolf planned. Now it was time for them to wait for the great detective to show up and solve the case.

CHAPTER ELEVEN

Front Step, Glenbogle Manor, Scottish Highlands, Scotland

Paris and Sophia both ran in toward the screams and commotion. The staff had all gathered around the body, and the sight was more gruesome than Paris had bargained for.

Ushering the maids and butlers back, Sophia tried to help to preserve the crime scene. To Paris' shock, Ramy had died…in the basement.

They found his body at the bottom of the basement stairs that led to the living quarters set up for the blue dragon and Sophia. Stranger still, Ramy's body was cut in several places, his clothes torn, and the grossest part was his impalement on a sword. Not just any sword, though.

Ramy Vance appeared to have been killed by Sophia Beaufont's sword—Inexorabilis.

Called by a servant, Rudolf ran down to the basement wearing a silk robe. His eyes darted to the dead body, then to Paris. He sort of smiled but she shook her head.

Still, he threw his hands up and yelled, "There's been muuuuurder."

She pointed at the sword. "Someone killed Ramy with Sophia's sword."

"That's not all." Sophia checked the backs of Ramy's legs and his back. "It appears something hit him."

Rudolf searched the space—the stairs behind them, the cozy, dark, dank basement around them, and the space on the first floor where the servants and guests had gathered. "I think there's much more to unravel here than what meets the eye. I simply don't know where to start. If only we had a way of deducing the clues…"

"Ru…" Paris warned, hoping he wasn't laying it on too thick.

"I mean, we can't call the authorities until morning," Rudolf continued. "At that point, some of the clues could've gone cold, about like Ramy's body. If only someone could tell us what happened here."

"Maybe we just wait…" Sophia offered.

"Yeah, and maybe we give up on life," Rudolf said melodramatically. "That's what we should probably do because I'm guessing there's no way we can solve this crime."

"I don't know what happened." Lunis peered at the stairs.

"Yeah, and I'm sure no one else does either," Rudolf continued. "I'm certain that no one can solve this case. It's too difficult because so many wanted Ramy dead and there's no way we can determine who did this."

"Uncle, I think you're laying it on a bit too—"

To Paris' shock, a figure emerged from the shadows of a basement corner, striding forward with a confident expression.

"I think I can help," the strange man in a dark trench coat with a hat and pipe said as he reached the body and looked down.

They all knew who he was. Paris' heart beat fast. By the look on Sophia's and Rudolf's and even Lunis' faces, their blood was pumping fast too.

Rudolf spoke first. "Who are you?"

The man turned, showing his face. A deerstalker cap partially obscured it, but still, Paris made out his strong features and clever smile. He pulled the pipe from his mouth, and something lit up his eyes. "I think you know. I wouldn't be a great detective if I didn't know that you lured me here with a complex mystery. But well done because it worked."

"So you don't know who killed Ramy Vance?" Paris was surprised.

The man shook his head. "No, but I'm going to find out because I'm Sherlock Holmes and there's no case I can't solve."

CHAPTER TWELVE

Basement, Glenbogle Manor, Scottish Highlands, Scotland

Of course, Paris wanted to tell Sherlock Holmes that he didn't have to waste his time finding Ramy's murderer because the man would soon awake from his non-death. However, she could tell by how the great detective was studying the body and crime scene that he was taking this all very seriously, and interrupting his process wouldn't do her any good.

She wanted Sherlock to help her, which meant she had to stay on his good side. Still, it was surreal to realize that she was watching the real Sherlock Holmes work a case as he took in every detail in the basement, smelling the air, licking the dust from his fingertips, and measuring various spots with his feet.

"I don't think Ramy will wake up until we remove the sword from him," Rudolf offered, pointing at the dead body. "I've been at enough of his deaths to know this."

"You can't tamper with a crime scene," Sherlock Holmes said at once, his expression all no-nonsense. "The sword stays."

"Okay, but you know that Ramy isn't truly dead, right?" Rudolf asked. "He's got a weird fountain of youth magic that prevents him from dying. So…"

"This is a crime scene," Sherlock stated, his British accent elegant but his words terse. "We don't tamper with it until I've solved the case."

Rudolf saluted. "You got it, chief." Then he turned to Sophia. "You can't have your sword until we find the murderer… Wait, your sword impaled Ramy…in the basement, where you were staying…"

"It wasn't me!" Sophia argued at once. "I was with Paris the entire night."

Paris nodded. "She was. I mean, except when she left to put her sword away, complaining that it was bothering her."

"Oh, how very convenient." Rudolf shook his head with disgust.

"I can't believe you think I could be a part of this." Sophia crossed her arms. "I came here to support Paris."

"And not because Ramy was skimming money off the till at Heals Pills and you knew about it and wanted to punish him," Rudolf condemned.

Sophia gasped. "I didn't know about that." Heals Pills was co-owned by her and Rudolf. It made sense that she'd be interested in the business, but not that she'd kill Ramy over something so small. Especially since his death would accomplish nothing for her. Unlike some, Sophia didn't care about vengeance.

Rudolf stroked his chin, nodding. "This has all been very enlightening, and I'm closer to solving this case."

"Would you stay out of my way?" Sherlock turned his attention to Paris and Sophia. "I need to examine the body and investigate the first floor. Last, I'll question the suspects, but until then, have them sequestered to their rooms alone."

He glanced back and pointed at Rudolf. "Will you keep this one out of my case? I can't have it tampered with."

They both nodded in reply to the detective. Paris was giddy, thinking that they'd done what they needed. However, she hadn't gotten Sherlock Holmes to help her find Subfar yet so the real mission was still on the horizon.

Pulling out her phone, she checked it to find no messages from Faraday—which meant that any new information on the big mission was still a long way off. Hopefully soon, they'd bust both cases wide open and make tons of progress.

Sherlock gave her a strange look before turning, his long trench coat sweeping behind him as he centered his attention squarely on Ramy's dead body.

CHAPTER THIRTEEN

Basement, Glenbogle Manor, Scottish Highlands, Scotland

It was like something out of a movie to watch Sherlock Holmes examining a dead body—working a murder case. Paris stood nearby so if the great detective needed any help, she could be of assistance. She was no John Watson, but she liked to think that she could help, offering insights or somehow fanning the flames of Sherlock's intelligence.

Sophia had gone upstairs with Rudolf to send everyone to their room until it was time for questions.

"Are you wondering why we lured you out of hiding with this case?" Paris dared to ask Sherlock as he stooped low, using a ballpoint pen to inspect the legs of Ramy's pants where there were several holes.

"I am a man of great intelligence and calculated decision-making." Sherlock didn't take his eyes off the body. "I do not wonder about things."

"Oh, but you said you knew that we got you here with a complex mystery, right? How is it that you figured it out?"

Sherlock rose to his feet, starting to walk around the body.

"You know, it is better to remain silent and be thought a fool than to speak and remove all doubt."

Paris tried not to let her embarrassment show on her face. She was used to being criticized by people, but not by Sherlock Holmes. Somehow his remarks cut her in a way she wasn't used to.

"Right, well, Dr. Watson knew we were looking for him, so I guess you have similar Spidey-senses."

Sherlock glanced at her, surprise in his dark eyes. "You spoke to Watson?"

Paris nodded. "He's the one who gave me the idea for how to find you. Watson said that you couldn't resist solving a good murder mystery. However, he didn't know where to find you."

Sherlock nodded, his gaze falling to the floor. "No, he wouldn't. I haven't seen him in quite some time."

"Do you miss your old partner?" Paris saw regret surface on his face.

Sherlock put his pipe in his mouth and bit down on it but didn't answer.

"Watson said that he'd tired of working cases but you never would," Paris continued, being bolder with her observations although she didn't know why. She didn't want to anger Sherlock. She wanted him to help her. But for some reason unknown to her, it made sense to have this conversation.

"I would miss oxygen for the one hundred and eighty seconds I was without it before my death," Sherlock began, striding around to Ramy's feet. "I would miss water for the seventy-two hours I was without it before my death. And I'd miss food—"

"I think I get the point," Paris interrupted, shaking her head, wondering if Sherlock was simply a big jerk.

"The point is," he continued, "that I miss things that sustain my life due to my human instinct to survive. However, I do not miss people or objects of personal interest or places full of rubbish things like nostalgia."

"221B Baker Street burned down," Paris lied.

Something small flickered across Sherlock's face. A rogue emotion that he didn't quell before rearranging his mask so that he didn't show any feelings on his face. "No, it didn't."

"But you'd miss it if it did," Paris stated with conviction.

Sherlock studied the bottoms of Ramy's feet before rising once more. "Miss Beaufont—"

"Agent Beaufont," she corrected, remembering that they hadn't exchanged names. The great detective seemed to know who she was and who knew what else he understood. Probably more than she'd care to know.

"Agent Beaufont," he continued. "It's evident that you have a calculated manner. Although I respect that, do not think I'm a case you can work. I don't need to be fixed by a fairy godmother. I don't miss Watson. I'm perfectly content with working cases on my own."

Paris nodded. "Well, then you're stronger than me. My partner is on another case, and I wish he were here. We complement each other. He sees things I don't and vice versa. I can always depend on him."

"A good partner is undoubtedly an asset." Sherlock strode around to where Ramy's face lay flat on the floor.

It was still surreal to Paris to think she was simply standing beside a dead body having a casual conversation with Sherlock Holmes. However, it helped if she didn't look at the blood-drenched sword protruding through his front and out the other side. The hilt made Ramy's body lie awkwardly, but it gave Sherlock a better way to inspect the body without touching it.

"Do you know who killed Ramy?" Paris watched as the great detective leaned closer, inspecting his face.

Sherlock took a handkerchief from his pocket and used it like a glove to move Ramy's face to the side. He then used a corner of the cloth to swab Ramy's lips before bringing it to his face. Paris wasn't sure what he would do, but she was relieved when he simply sniffed the handkerchief before slipping it back into his jacket.

"There is still much investigation to happen here."

"So no light at the end of the tunnel, then?"

Sherlock's gaze connected with Paris'. "Be careful about looking for light at the end of the tunnel. That light could just be an oncoming train."

"Huh?"

Sherlock stood, still studying the body. "A great detective doesn't long to get to the end of a tunnel. That would be working a case for the wrong reasons. A detective's job is to find out what happened from start to finish, not just how it ended, which is invariably with a murder. If you are only ever looking for the murderer, you will miss much of what transpired. The key to solving a mystery lies in the details."

"Oh, that makes sense." Paris watched as Sherlock came around to the other side of the body, kneeling once more and running his hand over Ramy's shoulder. "So he died from being stabbed with Sophia's sword…"

In a series of quick movements, Sherlock stood, pivoted, and faced her directly. "No, which is why you can't simply accept things at face value. He was dead before being stabbed."

"Oh, wow." Paris was shocked to hear this revelation, which complicated things.

"This case is far from straightforward, and it is far from over." Sherlock marched straight for the stairs, leaving Paris wishing that this didn't have to be so complicated. She wanted to get back to check on Faraday. Also, not until this case was over could she ask for Sherlock's help with finding Subfar.

When he was halfway up the stairs, the detective turned and glared down at Paris, giving her a pointed look. "Are you coming? I can work alone, but I'd prefer not to if a suitable partner is available."

CHAPTER FOURTEEN

First Floor Corridor, Glenbogle Manor, Scottish Highlands, Scotland

Had Sherlock Holmes paid her a compliment? Paris wondered as she joined him at the top of the basement stairs in Glenbogle Manor.

She reasoned that it wasn't the biggest of compliments if anything. The great detective had alluded that she was a suitable partner. Not a great one or a brilliant one, but suitable. And she was simply available, which meant he had limited options.

However, Sherlock had also stated that she had a "calculated manner," which sounded like a compliment. Paris had to remind herself that this was coming from the very unemotional Sherlock Holmes, who was as warm and fuzzy as a hacksaw.

The detective squatted to inspect the banister and balusters at the top of the staircase to the basement. He ran his fingers over some score marks on the wood. Where the railing and other stairs parts were damaged, splinters of wood protruded.

Sherlock glanced up at her with a speculative expression. "These marks are fresh."

"How can you tell?"

"The exposed wood is fresh in color, and the splinters are

sticking out," he explained. "If much time had gone by, foot traffic would mash the fibers of the splintered wood back down. Ironically, it is time that covers scars and damage—making them fade. Fresh ones stick out like a sore thumb."

"That is ironic and poetic," Paris observed.

Sherlock nodded, looking around, studying the many marks of damage on the stairs, banister, and balusters.

"That damage." Paris indicated the many scratch marks she saw now that she was looking. "Is it from Ramy falling down the stairs to the basement?"

He shook his head, pulled out his pipe again, and chewed on the stem but never smoked it. "No, someone pushed him, I believe."

"Oh." Paris looked around for more clues. That's when she noticed a small hole in the wall a few feet from the staircase landing. "Is that…a bullet hole?"

Sherlock followed her gaze, narrowing his eyes when he saw the damaged part of the wall. He strode over and reached up to touch the spot. It was nearly too high for him to reach although the detective was quite tall. He pulled his fingers from the wall, having retrieved a bullet from the hole. He sniffed it, rolling the small pea-shaped object around in his hand.

"Does it smell fresh?" Paris didn't know much about guns but thought that a recently fired bullet would have the scent of gunpowder.

"Yes, but it also smells of blood."

Paris' brow wrinkled in confusion. "Blood? How is that possible? Someone would have to be taller than you to get shot up there."

Sherlock shook his head. "The shooter didn't fire straight on. Instead, they shot at an angle."

"An angle?" Paris didn't understand what had happened here.

The detective glanced around the corridor. Seeming to get an idea, he strode to the far side of the area, looking up at where the bullet hole was a few yards from the basement staircase.

He squatted and squinted up, his brain undoubtedly calculating angles and several other factors. Watching him work was fascinating. Paris marveled at how he observed the scene, seeing it behind a magnifying glass. Just by being in his presence, she felt more focused than usual. She felt like her IQ had risen. It was exhilarating to be around the great detective. Suddenly she was baffled at how Watson wouldn't want to forever work cases alongside Sherlock Holmes.

This thought reminded her of Faraday, and she pulled her phone from her pocket, hoping to see a message from him. There wasn't one. She frowned. When she put her phone back in her pocket, she spied Sherlock studying her, his gaze dissecting her.

Before she could make an excuse for checking her phone, he pointed at the archway that led to the dining room and kitchen area of the manor. "Ramy came from there."

Paris nodded. "Yes, that would be correct. He'd been in the dining room before his death."

Sherlock shook his head. "Not only the dining room. He'd gone somewhere else before falling down the stairs."

"Oh, where?" Paris questioned, following the detective around the corner and down the hallway.

"I have an idea, but first I want to know how that happened." Sherlock halted, pointing at something inside the dining room. A silver tray lay on the floor. Its contents, a set of crystal goblets and a bottle of red wine, had shattered everywhere. The broken pieces of crystal and red wine mixed on the wood floor, making an artful and sinister arrangement.

CHAPTER FIFTEEN

Dining Room, Glenbogle Manor, Scottish Highlands, Scotland

Since Paris remembered hearing the crashing and breaking sounds before Ramy's death, she knew precisely who would know how the wine bottle and goblets got broken.

"That was me." Rudolf looked rather sheepish at being called in for questioning. He indicated the mess. "I dropped the tray, breaking its contents on the floor. I was trying to clean it up when one of the servants found Ramy's body and alerted us to the murder."

"Where were you taking the tray?" Sherlock studied the dining room table, which the servants still hadn't cleared after dinner due to all the activity in the house. Dirty dishes, empty wine bottles, and glasses littered it.

"I was taking it to my wife's quarters, although she'd asked me to stay away for the night."

Paris instantly felt bad for the king, whose Serena often shunned him. However, her pity was short-lived when a crooked smile formed on Rudolf's face.

"I figured she'd tell me to leave her alone," the fae explained. "Then I'd get credit for trying and could retire to my room to watch *Gossip Girl* in peace and drink the bottle of wine without sharing. Serena always spoils the show by asking questions."

"So you didn't want to spend the night with your wife?" Paris questioned.

"I know this will surprise you, but my lovely wife isn't that smart," Rudolf admitted.

Paris gasped. "Shocking."

Rudolf nodded. "I realize that you'd expect me to be with a nuclear rocket scientist brain surgeon, but alas, I chose a woman who was all heart and no brains."

"I think you meant all chest," Paris corrected.

"You dropped the tray because something startled you," Sherlock stated, looking between the dropped contents and the swinging door to the kitchen. He pointed. "Something that came from there. What was it?"

Rudolf's jaw dropped. "Wow, you're good. How did you know?"

"Even if I told you how I deduced such information, it would simply go over your head."

"Well," Rudolf said, narrowing his eyes at the detective. "If I told you how I use mind control, it would go over your head."

"You should use more mind control and less talking," Sherlock offered.

"Yes, but people always expect me to speak with such fluency as the king of the fae."

"Which is why you should keep the false reputation." Sherlock picked up a bottle of wine and sniffed the top. "Light travels faster than sound, which is why some people appear bright until you hear them speak."

Paris gave Rudolf a sympathetic look. "He insulted me for opening my mouth too. I think it's his thing."

Sherlock put the bottle down, picked up an empty wine goblet, and sniffed its rim. "A closed mouth gathers no foot."

"So, what startled you?" Paris asked Rudolf, ignoring Sherlock. "Why did you drop the tray?"

"Oh, it was Serena." Rudolf had forgotten where they were in the discussion. "I thought she was in her room, so I was surprised to find her in the kitchen. Well, really, I would be surprised to find my wife in any kitchen, ever. She must have been lost in this large mansion and thought it was the wine cellar."

"Why would seeing your wife startle you so much that you dropped the tray?" Sherlock ran his finger over the tabletop and inspected the tip with a studious expression.

"Well, like I said, I expected her to be in her room," Rudolf explained. "But it was the murderous expression on her face. It was the one she gives me when I've gotten away with something, and she's plotting how to get back at me. However, I hadn't done anything…well, besides being born and breathing, as she likes to put it."

"She sounds ever so charming." Sherlock pointed around the table where the various empty wine bottles were. "Even though your wife likes wine, it wasn't her who emptied these."

"That was a statement rather than a question," Rudolf stated. "I don't understand, and I'm a very educated person."

Sherlock shook his head. "I doubt that you are, but regardless, education is rubbish in this world. Knowledge is knowing a tomato is a fruit. Wisdom is not putting it in a fruit salad."

"Wisdom is not eating a fruit salad." Rudolf grimaced.

"Yes, I'm stating that your wife wasn't the one who drank this wine." Sherlock waved at the table. "Who was it?"

"Honestly, I don't know," Paris admitted. "When we got to dinner, there were a bunch of half-empty and empty bottles of wine on the table. Our glasses were full, and I assumed the staff had taken care of everything."

"Yes, because waitstaff are known for leaving empty wine bottles on tables," Sherlock stated sarcastically.

"What are you saying?" Paris asked.

"I'm not saying anything yet." Sherlock turned and trudged for the kitchen, his trench coat like a cape flying up behind him from his movement as he swept from the room.

Rudolf glanced at Paris and rolled his eyes. "Is that dude all drama or what?"

"I think he likes to make an exit, for sure."

"He can hear you," Sherlock called from the kitchen. "Dear Paris, get in here at once."

CHAPTER SIXTEEN

Kitchen, Glenbogle Manor, Scottish Highlands, Scotland

Paris wasn't sure what she expected when she followed Sherlock into the manor's kitchen. Maybe a giant clue sitting in the open, waiting for them to record it. What she found wasn't anything of particular interest.

"What is this?" She looked around the large space with tons of cabinets, counter space, utensils, and cooking surfaces.

"A kitchen," he said simply, opening various cabinets and drawers and inspecting them.

"Why thanks, but no shit, Sherlock..." Paris froze, looked up at the old detective, and gave him a nervous smile.

She was utterly surprised when he chuckled. "That's a good one."

"You haven't heard that before?"

"I haven't heard a lot before," he stated. "I stay buried in my work if that's not evident."

"Okay, well, when the kids these days make fun of each other, they say things like, 'No shit, Sherlock...'" She stopped, getting the impression that he wasn't paying attention. Paris watched as he swept his eyes over the kitchen, inspecting a drawer or cupboard before moving to the pantry and the walk-in freezer, which would have been a new addition when the owner modernized the manor.

When he returned, Sherlock put his hands on his hips and glanced at her. "What do you see?"

"What am I looking for?"

"You are always looking for the mundane, the simple things, but it will be slightly out of place. A butter knife where butter knives don't go. A cabinet a bit open, meaning that it was recently in use. A crumb or something that means someone was eating without a plate."

"Is that the crime here then?" she said facetiously. "Are we policing etiquette?"

"What is out of place here, Paris?"

"I don't know." Paris felt put on the spot as she looked around, her heart beating loudly suddenly. She pointed at a knife lying on a cutting board. "Is it that?"

"What?" he asked, seemingly entertained by this. "A knife on a cutting board? How out of place is that?"

"I don't know," she repeated. "Apparently, I'm failing at this little game we're playing."

"If you try to fail and succeed, which have you done?" he asked seriously.

Paris shook her head. "Apparently, I'm a bad detective and need more education."

He shook his head, stalking back toward the dining room. Before leaving, he whipped around, facing her with a critical expression. "Your problem isn't education. It is that no one's ever taught you how to look at something. Really see it as it is.

"Instead, you fill in the details with how you expect them to look. You search for the things that are in their place instead of the ones that are out of place. If you're going to be a good detective, you have to stop entering every situation and looking at it with filters and instead see what *is* there. I'm a smart man, but it's only because I see what's there when the rest of the world sees what they want."

He flicked his hand to the kitchen. "Now, go ahead and look again at the kitchen and tell me, what do you see? If you have no expectations, if you're not filling it in with what you *think* will be there, what's truly there? What do you see?"

Paris hesitated before turning and studying the space around her. At first, her eyes homed in on the mundane—the sink, the stove, the dirty dishes, and the used kitchen towels. Then she wiped that from her mind and saw things as they were. The unexpected shone through as though highlighted, like someone had circled them in red ink. Like they had been lined up on an evidence sheet for a murder—making a solid case.

CHAPTER SEVENTEEN

Sitting Room, Glenbogle Manor, Scottish Highlands, Scotland

"This is ridiculous!" Serena Sweetwater protested, stomping across the elegantly appointed sitting room at the front of Glenbogle Manor.

Sherlock Holmes had requested that all the guests gather together while he reviewed his notes after completing his full investigation and questioning everyone.

Paris thought she knew what had occurred that night, thanks to the opportunity to shadow Sherlock. However, there were still unclear details. The fact that the detective had unraveled it all from the clues was impressive. If anything, Paris thought she could only understand what happened because she knew the characters involved. And yet, there were a few things she was waiting to learn from the great detective.

"Honey, I told you that I'd buy you a Savannah cat from Africa to make up for all this stress," Rudolf offered, patting the space next to him on the couch, encouraging his wife to come and sit next to him.

"But one of those creatures will eat Captain Silver." Serena paused her pacing to consider this offer.

Rudolf paused too. "Do you mean our daughter, Captain Silver, or that dog?" He pointed at the creature shivering in the corner, who Paris was pretty sure had piddled on the antique rug.

"I mean the dog," Serena stated. "Our daughter is Sailor from now on."

"I think the jury is still out on that, dear." Rudolf had encouraged Serena to join him and pulled her to him.

"I don't like being locked up with all of you murderers." Bep sat in the opposite corner and clutched her potions bag on her lap. Paris hadn't noticed it on her person when she arrived and guessed it was under her traveling cloak.

"Only one of you is a murderer," Lunis corrected, curled up next to his rider and pretty much taking up half of the large space having used a compartment spell to fit in the room. "So if it makes anyone feel better, we can't trust one of you soulless jerks."

Sophia shook her head. "I really can't believe that one of you murdered Ramy. I mean, I get that he can come back to life and is pretty insufferable and smells like cheese, but you killed your friend."

"He's not my friend," Serena said at once. Rudolf patted her on the shoulder, pulling her back in and calming her from the sudden outburst.

"Nor mine." Bep shook her head.

Quiet mumbled from the corner next to the door.

From the fourth corner, looking out the window at the dark moor, Paris shook her head. There was a dead man down in the basement, three bickering lunatics, and a lot more problems for her to unravel. She'd successfully gotten Sherlock there, but something about him challenged her in new ways.

"What's her problem?" Bep pointed in her direction.

"Have you considered that it's you?" Serena asked.

"Have you considered that it's you're egocentric and the ruiner of this festive affair?" Bep shot back.

"A lot of people say that I'm egocentric," Lunis said matter-of-factly. "But really, enough about them."

"Do you ever stop?" Sophia asked her dragon.

He shook his head. "I'm helping the mood. Everyone is acting so depressed."

"A man is dead," Paris remarked.

"You pull out the sword, and he's back," Lunis offered.

"Yeah, but that's the problem with this world, isn't it?" Paris began. "We believe that we can kill someone, and it doesn't matter because it's not real, but what does it do to us at the core? And we watch a show and forget about the real ones in our lives. The same thing happens with social media and video games. We're all living these unreal lives where nothing matters, and the real problem is that we're out of touch."

"Someone is letting it all out." Bep shook her head in disapproval.

"Yeah, get a therapist," Serena insulted.

"I need a new therapist," Lunis interjected. "Mine says that I have a preoccupation with vengeance." He narrowed his eyes and issued smoke from his nostrils. "We'll see about that..."

Sophia groaned. "At this point, I'm thinking of killing myself to get away from these bad jokes."

Paris shook her head. "I think we all need to have a moment of silence to show our respect to Ramy. Also, one of you killed him, and while you won't get punished when he comes back to life, you need to atone for what you've done. Also, I'll be keeping an eye on you little creeps."

"That's a good idea," Rudolf stated. "Even if that little annoyance is coming back to life, we should still show some respect for another death he's suffered."

"And while we're quiet, whoever killed him, think about what you did and how you disrespected a human life." Paris felt only marginally guilty about setting all this up. However, she only invited those who she thought would commit the crime and one of them proved her right.

"Yeah, I think taking a moment to grieve is a good idea." Sophia faintly smiled at Paris, giving her some encouragement.

"You know, I had the best grief counselor I could've recommended," Lunis imparted thoughtfully.

"You could have?" Rudolf asked. "Why can't you?"

"Oh, because he died," Lunis answered. "But he was so good at his job that I didn't care."

Everyone in the room groaned in response this time.

However, they all fell immediately silent when Sherlock Holmes burst into the room, standing on the threshold in his deerstalker and trench coat, pipe in hand, and glint of knowing in his eyes.

"I know exactly how Ramy Vance was murdered…"

CHAPTER EIGHTEEN

Sitting Room, Glenbogle Manor, Scottish Highlands, Scotland

Paris held her breath when the great detective entered the sitting room and strode into the middle of the space. She'd figured out a lot of what had happened to Ramy with Sherlock's guidance. She thought she knew what had happened in the kitchen, the dining room, and on the staircase landing. However, there were still a few unclear details.

Everyone straightened as Sherlock commanded the space with his presence and the studious glint in his eyes. No one made a noise.

"It wasn't one of you who murdered Ramy Vance," Sherlock Holmes began, looking around the group, his eyes connecting with all suspects—Bep, Quiet, and Queen Serena Sweetwater. Everyone held in gasps, disbelieving this news. He then pointed around the room at the three. "It was all of you."

Then, to Paris' shock, Sherlock also pointed at Sophia and Lunis.

Sophia stood, shaking her head. "I didn't kill Ramy. Lunis either... We're innocent."

"Your involvement was simply a case of negligence," Sherlock stated, "but your dragon has a very heavy hand in this murder and is as culpable as the others for this crime, although his would be considered more manslaughter than premeditated."

Sophia turned to her dragon, thoroughly confused and shocked, probably hoping that he'd tell her that the detective was wrong. To her surprise and Paris', Lunis had his head buried in his clawed paws.

"Lunis?" Sophia asked.

"I can explain." Lunis' voice came out muffled.

"Allow me," Sherlock began, pacing with his hands behind his back. He made his way to one side of the sitting room and the other. "This case ends with the blue dragon, but it begins much earlier."

Paris straightened and looked at Rudolf, who shared her dual emotions of excitement and nervousness.

Sherlock paused in front of Bep, giving her a cunning glare. "Now, you, the potions maker, had a grievance with the deceased so you put one of your poison potions into his wine. However, he wasn't drinking in the music room. So you left early, went into the dining room, and put the poison into his soup, teacup, and wine, knowing that one way or another, he'd get the dose. Being drunk by that point, you left many of the empty wine bottles on the table before stumbling to your room. Am I correct?"

Bep hung her head, looking remorseful. "I didn't want him ruining my weekend with his loudness and smiling."

"Understood. I've had many a weekend ruined by such things. Happy people are the worst."

"So it was Bep?" Paris asked. "But you said that it wasn't one of them. She poisoned Ramy, and he fell down the stairs."

"Not quite," Sherlock stated. "Remember the kitchen."

"Yes, but I don't know exactly what I saw there except that something wasn't right," Paris explained. "There was a weird powder on the floor and the walls around the freezer. Honestly, I would have noticed if I was looking. But I wasn't, like you said."

"Precisely," Sherlock trumpeted, continuing to pace. "While Bep was busy putting poison in the wine, Serena set the stage for her own murder. She was busy hiding in the kitchen until dinner was over. When she heard you all leaving, she quietly waved Ramy into the kitchen with some bogus request."

"I told him I found cookies," Serena offered.

"Good one, dear," Rudolf gushed. "That one always works."

"Ramy, still hungry and the poisoned wine starting to hit him, staggered to the kitchen," Sherlock continued. "That's where Serena tried to lock him into the walk-in freezer, also hoping to get rid of him for the weekend."

"He's such an annoyance," Serena stated.

Rudolf nodded. "Imagine working with the guy."

"Oh, so you don't like it?" Serena asked.

"Of course not. He does all the grunt work, darling."

"However," Sherlock cut in, "Ramy realized what was happening before Serena got the freezer locked. She struggled with it, not used to working such things like freezers, locks, or doors."

"They're so complicated," Serena complained.

Rudolf nodded. "I hear that."

"Although he was drugged, Ramy broke free from the compartment and made his way out of the freezer," Sherlock explained.

"But he was limping, and his feet were covered in dry ingredients stored in the freezer," Paris nearly exclaimed, remembering seeing the weird marks that looked like footprints on the floor but not sure exactly what they were. "And there were things like handprints on the walls around the freezer."

It made sense they were left by a drugged person now. Looking at the case from the beginning was starting to make a lot more sense than only looking for the murderer. Otherwise, one would miss a lot.

"Exactly." A hint of approval entered Sherlock's voice as he stopped pacing in front of Quiet. "And you, the groundskeeper for the Dragon Elite, planned to shoot Ramy in cold blood when he went up to his room, an act of revenge that would make you feel better and not last for the man who can't die."

"Easily," Rudolf added. "Ramy can't die easily."

"Right," Sherlock stated. "But Quiet, who is an excellent shot and wouldn't usually miss, very practiced as a ghillie, did miss hitting a vital organ. He managed to shoot Ramy, but only in the shoulder because he was spooked by the commotion when you, Rudolf, dropped the tray because Serena ran out of the kitchen going after Ramy, who had escaped the freezer."

Rudolf nodded. "I'd brought the tray and wine in from the hall. Then I saw Serena, and she looked upset about something, and I was surprised to see her in the kitchen so I dropped the tray with the glasses and wine."

"At precisely the moment Quiet was aiming," Sherlock continued. "Making him miss slightly. However, he still shot his man, making Ramy yelp, but the disturbance with the breaking glass drowned out all the noise in the dining room. But someone heard it and ran to see what was happening."

Everyone looked around, trying to figure out who Sherlock was referring to. All their gazes settled on the great detective with hungry expressions.

"The dragon heard what had transpired and hoping to come to the rescue, bounded into the hallway able to enter due to a compartment spell that shrinks dragons. However, due to Ramy's bad luck, Lunis' tail whipped across the space and knocked into the injured and drugged man who was mostly dead already, sending him down the stairs to his death."

"That's how the stairs got damaged," Paris said aloud, putting it all together.

Sherlock nodded. "Ramy tumbled to the bottom of the stairs where he knocked Sophia's sword from its place propped against the wall and was impaled upon it, really ending him."

For a full minute, the room fell silent.

Finally, Rudolf spoke. "Well, I'm sleeping with my door locked tonight."

"I don't think any of you would have murdered if it wasn't Ramy," Paris amended.

"He brings out the worst in people," Serena stated.

Paris shook her head. "No, you killed a man who can't easily die. I'm not sure that if the act isn't permanent that it detracts from what you did. So I think you all should take the rest of the weekend to think about this. We need to be accountable to each other, but more importantly to ourselves. We should be taking care of each other."

"Paris is right." Sophia patted Lunis on the side. "Don't worry, big guy. You didn't mean to knock Ramy down the stairs. You were trying to help."

"But I didn't tell you because I didn't want to go to jail," Lunis wailed.

"On that note, I think I'll go to bed." Bep rose to her feet and made her way to the door.

"Fine," Rudolf chirped. "But leave the bag of potions, murderer."

Bep rolled her eyes but left her bag on the table before exiting.

Quiet muttered something inaudible as he left the sitting room.

Serena was mostly talking to herself too when she left carrying her dog, Captain Silver.

"I think we better go and retrieve your sword, Sophia." Rudolf stretched as he stood. "Then we'll welcome Ramy back to the world."

Sophia nodded, encouraging Lunis out of the sitting room first before she followed. "Yes, but I don't think we should tell him that he was the victim of multiple attempts on his life tonight."

"Agreed." Rudolf allowed her to exit first and followed her out, leaving Paris and Sherlock alone in the sitting room to discuss one last thing.

CHAPTER NINETEEN

Sitting Room, Glenbogle Manor, Scottish Highlands, Scotland

"I have to say, Agent Beaufont, that I've worked a lot of cases, but I haven't had…dare I say this much enjoyment, doing so in quite some time." Sherlock's gaze felt like it was cutting into her as she stood a few feet from the man before her.

"Well, Rudolf throws a good party," she muttered.

"I work cases out of necessity as I'm sure Watson alluded to," Sherlock went on like he hadn't heard her. "But I don't derive pleasure from them. Not like I used to. However, on this occasion, I sort of enjoyed some elements."

"The eccentric socialite? The crazy potions lady? The mostly mute gnome?" Paris wagered.

"It was probably the blue dragon." Sherlock almost smiled. "I also appreciate when I can work with someone who brings out my brilliance."

Paris sort of smiled too. "Watson said something about that. About how his slowness made your intelligence grow brighter."

Sherlock chuckled. "That sounds like something Watson would say."

"Well, as you might have deduced, I lured you here because I've discovered that you can help me with an important case."

Sherlock nodded. "I might be able to."

"Anyway, can you…will you help me with my case? It's a huge mystery, that only you can solve," Paris stated. "My partner, Faraday, has gone missing. I don't know where to look, but I must find him. I'll pay you whatever it takes to get him back."

"I don't want your money." Sherlock scoffed. "But I will take your case."

"Thank you," Paris gushed, relief flooding her chest. She felt like she could finally breathe, but only a little.

"Of course. And I understand. A good partner is worth worrying about," Sherlock said. "We need to follow the clues, find your partner, and solve this case with efficiency. How does that sound?"

Paris nodded, grateful that she'd drawn Sherlock Holmes out of hiding and that he'd agreed to help. Now she had the best and the brightest detective to help her find Faraday. Her partner was the best and the brightest, so it only seemed fitting.

MURDER IN A SMALL TOWN

CHAPTER ONE

Haunted Harbor, Maine, New England, United States

Agent Paris Beaufont's job had taken her on the strangest mission so far. She'd been sent to a place where some of the highest frequency levels of hate in the world had been recorded. That was key to finding something critical that Paris needed for her current mission. It was always one wild goose chase after another in her world. No case was straightforward. No solution found without piecing together several parts of a whole.

Paris needed a very important potion ingredient for her current mission. And that component could most easily be found in a certain place—one filled with hatred. Furthermore, it could only be harvested at a very specific time—just after a murder...

If the small sleepy village located off the Gulf of Maine was full of hate, then Paris might have misunderstood what the word actually meant. Standing on the boardwalk and looking out at the port of seaworthy vessels like cargo ships, much loved sailboats, ferries, and fishing boats, Paris couldn't help but think that Haunted Harbor was idyllic.

The morning sunlight glistening off the choppy water made her squint as she studied the inlet where they were situated.

There were tiny little islands that guarded the harbor from the rough waters of the Atlantic Ocean to the east.

Nestled on one of the islands covered in green grass and wildflowers was the cutest lighthouse that looked like something out of a painting. Puffy clouds hung in the sky overhead, framing it just perfectly. To complete the image, a sailboat cut across the water just in front of it, its sails whipping in the wind and its crew looking proud as they headed out of the safety of the harbor.

"Yeah, this place is just so evil, I can't stand it," Paris said to her companions, turning to take in the town with its shops and houses nestled on the hills above.

"I sense that to be sarcasm," Sherlock Holmes stated, his hands behind his back as he also studied their surroundings. "Don't be so quick to judge. Appearances can be deceptive. Oftentimes, hatred wears a mask. We will have to investigate more to find out why this place registered as having high levels of animosity and therefore a likely place for a murder."

Paris ran her eyes over the man beside her. "You're Sherlock Holmes. Don't murders follow you around?"

He regarded her under his flat hat. "If they did, I think that would make me a very suspicious character. No, I arrive when there is a mystery to be solved. I sense them the same way that some people are drawn to drama or adventure or whatever it might be."

"What did Father Time say?" King Rudolf asked.

"He said that this place was full of extreme levels of animosity," Paris began, pushing her blonde hair behind her ears. The New England wind worked against her efforts and tried to tangle it back in her face. "And that to get what we need for the potion, we had to come here and collect a sample of the water." She pointed to the harbor in front of them. "Since water shares the collective consciousness of the emotions around it, it would be at the highest potency after a certain event happened."

"A murder," Sherlock Holmes guessed.

"How do we know that one will happen?" the king of the fae asked.

"Because Papa Creola, none other than Father Time, told us," Paris answered. "If this place is full of extreme levels of animosity, then it's full of homicides."

Rudolf nodded, his blond hair catching in the wind. "What better place than a quiet fishing village in Maine. I mean, it is the ideal place to bury a body."

Paris glanced sideways at her uncle, giving him a questioning look. "You said that out loud."

He gasped, putting his hand on his chest. "Not for me to bury a body. I haven't done that in quite some time. I'm a king and a father now. I mean, sometimes the wife pushes my levels of inhibitions on that, but so far I'm maintaining a clean record."

Paris returned her attention to the cute little houses dotting the hill. They looked like great places to swing on a front porch or jump in leaves in the front yard. She didn't understand how a place like this was full of so much hate, but that's why she brought the great detective, Sherlock Holmes. King Rudolf was more of a tag along but would probably prove to be surprisingly helpful.

"I don't know, if this place is so bad, maybe I can get some cheap real estate here," Paris joked. "It seems so quaint and peaceful."

"Haunted Harbor doesn't have the nicest ring to it, though," Rudolf pointed out.

"People love things that are haunted," Paris related. "They go out of their way to stay in haunted hotels or houses. It's exciting and shows history. Besides, it's just a name."

Sherlock Holmes stood next to her, his dark eyes scanning the Main Street in front of them lined with shops. They weren't busy, but the town also didn't appear to be bustling with people. "At first glance, Haunted Harbor does appear to be very picturesque, but there's definitely more than meets the eye. Remember that everything you see is a clue."

Paris honed her eyes on the various shops, taking in anything of interest.

"What do you see?" Sherlock Holmes asked her, seeming to be testing her.

"The town is divided," Paris answered slowly, studying the signs in the different store windows. "It appears that each shop is either catering to tourists or locals, but not both."

Sherlock Holmes nodded proudly. "That's right." He indicated to Peggy's Pie Shop in front of them and the sign in the window. "All Pies Named After Locals."

Rudolf pointed to the Howell Inn and Eatery down the main street. "No Longer Serving Locals."

"And check out the Fish Fry." Paris nodded at the greasy looking restaurant at the end of the lane. A chalkboard sandwich board sign read: "To All Tourists: Our Food Isn't Poisoned. Ask a Local."

"Okay, that's just weird," King Rudolf said.

"I know, right? Like why is there such a rub between the locals and the tourists?" Paris asked.

"No, I was referring to that," King Rudolf replied.

Paris turned to find him pointing at a large and very shiny ship. The vessel that sailed into the harbor was filled with excited people. More importantly, it was unmistakably operated by pirates.

CHAPTER TWO

Haunted Harbor, Maine, New England, United States

Although the mast of the ship sailing across the harbor didn't have black sails with skulls and crossbones, it was clear it was a pirate's ship. The name across the side was Haunted Harbor's Pirate Tour. Also, the crew was all dressed in black pants, vests and boots, and white puffy shirts. The man standing at the mast wearing a large captain's jacket wore a black pirate's hat.

"I'm guessing those are all tourists," Paris observed as the ship sailed along the coast where the lighthouse was nestled. Beside it was another island with a large saltbox house, a regal lawn, a dock with a motor boat, and standing on it was a woman. From across the harbor, Paris spied the very beautiful woman standing on the end of the dock, staring out at the ship as it approached her mansion.

Paris' enhanced vision gave her details about the woman. She was dressed importantly in a tailored red dress and high heels. Her long brown hair was sleek and caught the wind, although the woman didn't seem to mind. Actually she appeared furious about something, but it didn't appear to be the wind. Her red lips were pursed, and she stuck her hands on her hips as a microphoned voice called from the ship.

"Ladies and gentlemen, we'll start our tour of Haunted Harbor with the witch who keeps the ghosts trapped here," the ship's captain said over a loudspeaker in a thick British accent. From the rails of the ship, tourists all leaned over the side to get a closer look at the woman in the red dress, who was definitely madder than hell. She didn't look like the witches Paris had met. "This is Rebecca Flores, but she's known as the Witch of the Ghosts. If you see her, look away for if you spy her double pupiled eyes then you yourself will become a ghost. The only way to keep her from using her dark magic on you is to sing the song *Puff the Magic Dragon*. Let's all do it together now. I'll start, in case you forgot the lyrics."

The pirates hummed three times loudly, staring intently at the woman on the peer whose eyes were little slits. Anger radiated from every part of her.

"Here we go," the captain began. All at once he and his crew began singing.

"Puff the magic dragon lived by the sea!"

The tourists all cheered, excited by the sudden song. They quickly joined in, singing along. "He frolicked in the autumn mist in a land called Honah Lee."

The beautiful woman didn't hear the rest of the song. At least not from her place on the pier. Instead, she spun around and stormed for the saltbox house and disappeared inside.

The singers exclaimed.

The captain whooped, throwing his fist into the air. "Great job! Now remember, once in Haunted Harbor if you see Rebecca Flores, you sing that song. Never look her in the double pupiled eyes, or else you'll be a ghost like so many who haunt our poor town."

The crowd awww'd and ohed at this, seeming to be hinged on the pirate's every word.

"Soon I'll take you to tour our cursed village," the pirate continued over the loudspeaker that echoed across the harbor.

The tourists all yelled with excitement.

The man held up his hand to pause them. "But first, we have to get you ready. Get you safe. Even once you're outfitted, you must follow my every word. Unless you want to become a permanent resident of Haunted Harbors. By that, I mean a ghost!"

"No!" the crowd all replied, looking at each other as the ship continued across the harbor.

"Then we set sail for Dagger Island!" the captain roared, his fist in the air. "There, we will prepare for our journey into the dangerous and deadly town of Haunted Harbors."

"Yeah!" the crazed tourists in windbreakers and with fanny packs all rejoiced.

Paris turned to Sherlock Holmes and King Rudolf, giving them a confused look. "We've got some investigating to do."

The fae nodded, winking at her. "The best way to learn about the locals is from their pie." He thumbed in the direction of Peggy's Pie Shop behind them.

"Good idea," Sherlock Holmes agreed. "No one will know more about them and the happenings here than someone who names her pies after locals."

"No, I mean eating the pies," Rudolf corrected, making for the steps to the restaurant. "I can tell you everything about a place from their key lime or rhubarb pie."

CHAPTER THREE

Peggy's Pie Shop, Haunted Harbor, Maine, New England, United States
The café was just as charming as the other parts of the town Paris had seen. There were cute china plates with pictures of birds, rabbits, or other woodland creatures hanging on the wall. All the tables were covered in hand-knitted tablecloths, and fresh flowers sat in the center in little vases.

"What are you all doing in here?" a woman with short red hair who resembled Lucille Ball and was wearing a waitress outfit asked.

Paris glanced behind them at the door they'd come through and pointed at the sign. "It says that you're open. Aren't you?"

"Of course I am," the woman replied, leaning to the side to look through the big picture window. "The tour ship hasn't come in yet. Where you from?"

"We're not from around here," Rudolf answered, sliding into a booth by the window with a view and grabbing a menu, not taking the hint they weren't welcome.

"Clearly," the woman said, her hands now on her hips. "So what are you playing at? Why are you in here?"

"To get pie!" Rudolf exclaimed, his eyes wide as he took in the options.

"But you're not from around here," the woman said sternly.

"I'm sensing that you don't serve tourists," Sherlock Holmes began. "Is that correct?"

"It's not that I don't," the woman told him. "It's they don't come in here."

"Why?" Paris asked.

The woman lifted an eyebrow, studying her leather jacket and pants, then Sherlock Holmes in his tweed coat and King Rudolf in his silk tunic and pants. "Where did you all come from?"

"The interstate…" Paris said, drawing out the words.

The woman shook her head. "That's closed. The only way in here is through the harbor. Why are you lying?"

"Why does no one come here?" Paris asked.

"Because it's haunted," the woman said severely.

Paris had so many questions she didn't even know where to begin. Based on the quizzical expression on Sherlock's face, he did too.

"So why did you lie to me?" the woman continued. "The only way in here is through magic or the harbor. One is allowed. The other isn't. So tell me, did you break the captain's rules?" She leaned forward and smiled for the first time. "Because if you did, I'm naming a pie after you."

CHAPTER FOUR

Peggy's Pie Shop, Haunted Harbor, Maine, New England, United States

"What are the captain's rules?" Sherlock Holmes asked, sliding into the booth opposite King Rudolf, not waiting for an invitation.

The woman rolled her bright green eyes. "There are too many to count. Specifically, he's the only one who can bring outsiders into Haunted Harbor, and only via boat. So how did you all get here? More importantly, why?"

Paris took the seat next to her uncle Rudolf. "We portaled. We're magicians and fairies. We came for...vacation."

The woman laughed. "No one comes here to vacation. They come here to explore. To gawk. To be entertained by the ghosts. No one in their right mind comes here to vacation."

"Because it's haunted?" King Rudolf asked, lowering the menu.

"Because the captain has seen to it," the waitress said. "No one in their right mind on the east coast ventures here. The port is closed to outside boats regardless. His crew sees to it."

"Because it's haunted?" Paris repeated the king's question.

The woman drew in a breath. "Why are you all here?"

Paris and Sherlock Holmes exchanged looks. They couldn't tell this woman that a murder would happen there, but they could tell her something akin to the truth. She gave the great detective a curt nod, and he took the hint, clearing his throat and spreading his hands across the table.

"We're investigators," Sherlock Holmes began. "We learned there were some problems in this area. They came up on our radar of sorts. Where there's a problem, we like to create solutions. So...Miss...?"

"Peggy," she supplied, pointing at the sign over the counter bar at the bar. "I'm Peggy of Peggy's Pies."

"So, Peggy," Sherlock Holmes continued. "Is there a problem in Haunted Harbor, and is there a way that three very talented investigators can help?"

She sighed and looked off through the window, her gaze heavy. When she returned her attention to them, she seemed hopeful. "There are so many problems. Whether you can help, that's to be determined. First, you're at Peggy's Pies. Order a slice, and then we'll talk. Everyone is always happier when they have a slice of my pie."

CHAPTER FIVE

Peggy's Pie Shop, Haunted Harbor, Maine, New England, United States
The slice of Maureen's maple walnut pie melted in Paris' mouth. She didn't usually care much for pies or sweets, really. That Peggy knew how to make pie was evidenced by the way Rudolf kept slapping the table.

"Mother father, this piece of Rebecca's rhubarb pie is the best thing I've ever had," the fae exclaimed, continuing to slap his hand on the table.

Peggy grinned, looking at Sherlock. "How about yours? Is it okay?"

The detective had only taken one bite of pie before pushing back in the booth like he had enough. He nodded. "This Harrison's huckleberry pie is divine. I just don't want to overdo it with something so indulgent."

Paris smiled at the woman. "Sherlock tends to be pretty conservative."

"Sherlock," the woman said, drawing out his name. "As in Sherlock Holmes? Like the real detective?"

Paris nodded. "We told you we were investigators. So can you please tell us about this captain and why he seems to rule over this place? He doesn't allow outside boats in the harbor. Why?"

"Because it's haunted," Rudolf answered for the woman. "Didn't you hear his speech? It's not safe. It sounds like Mr. Captain is trying to keep outsiders safe. As a father of three captains, I'll tell you they are managers. Protectors. Little dictators." He looked intently at Peggy. "Are you, the locals, not affected by the ghosts? Will you not be turned into one by that mean hottie in the red dress?"

Peggy edged Sherlock Holmes over, sitting in the booth next to him. "The problem with Haunted Harbors isn't that it's haunted—"

"It is?" Sherlock interrupted.

She nodded. "Of course. It's always been haunted. There's a cosmic energy here that makes it so spirits don't move on. Many who die in this town, but not all, turn into ghosts and just stay here, peacefully haunting. Who knows exactly why."

"Fascinating," Sherlock Holmes observed.

Paris made a mental note she had to tell Faraday about this, especially since they had that ghost problem in the basement of FGA. Or maybe it wasn't so much of a problem.

"The ghosts used to be believed to protect the town," Peggy continued, pinning her elbows on the table and leaning forward. "They've never hurt anyone. They are pretty much everywhere. For the longest time, they were a source of commerce for us. Tourists came from all over to stay in the Howell's Inn and sleep in one of the haunted bedrooms. Or rent one of the houses on the hill with a famous ghost who walks the grounds. All our businesses started booming because ghost hunters wanted to come here to learn about our dead residents." Her eyes narrowed. "A few months ago, that man took advantage of our uniqueness here in Haunted Harbor. By the time we figured it out, it was too late. We've been at his mercy ever since."

"The captain?" Paris asked, pointing out the window to where the boat had long since disappeared, apparently to Dagger Island.

Peggy nodded. "He calls himself Captain Salty Saul."

"Is he a pirate?" Rudolf asked.

"He's worse," Peggy said. "He's an opportunist with no soul. As a longtime resident here, Saul took advantage when his father passed, leaving him a mighty fine inheritance. His father had, like all of us, benefited from the economy our ghosts brought us via tourism. Upon receiving his money, Saul bought that boat, hired a crew, and created a massive advertising campaign for his brand new company. Haunted Harbor Pirate Tours."

"He sounds like a smart chap," Rudolf said, taking a bite of his pie.

Peggy shot him an angry look. "Look sugar, I'm not arguing that. He's also a soulless man who was out for revenge from the moment he had the means. He never wanted to stay here after moving here with his father. Saul Senior wouldn't grant his son the resources to move back to England. Saul Junior grew resentful of his time living in Haunted Harbor. More importantly, he grew resentful of the residents and started taking names. We had no idea he was working on a long plan to make us all suffer one day, the way he thought he had."

Paris pushed her pie away, not able to eat another bite. "I don't understand. So Saul bought a boat and crew and guards Haunted Harbor and doesn't allow outsiders to come here?"

"Oh, he allows outsiders in here," Peggy replied. "Only, on his terms. You see, he started this tour company, but he did this huge marketing campaign in all the big cities, and news spread it was unsafe to come here unless you were on Saul's boat. False rumors spread, by his design, of people who were turned into ghosts here. He invoked fear in everyone. In just a few short months, he's managed to control everything that happens in our town via the tourists. They do everything he says and believe every word he tells them, and the people he hates suffer. The ones he doesn't are allowed to profit, but only marginally."

"What about the people he likes?" Rudolf asked.

Peggy laughed at this. "Saul doesn't like anyone. He never has."

"That woman on the pier," Paris began, pointing out to the saltbox house that could be seen from their table. "We saw her earlier. What did he call her?"

"Rebecca Flores," Sherlock Holmes supplied.

"Witch of the Ghosts," King Rudolf added.

Peggy shook her head. "Rebecca is no witch. The poor dear has it harder than the rest of us. Saul mostly hit us financially, but he attacks her daily at the heart."

"He humiliated her," Paris said. "I thought it was part of some show. What happened?"

"Saul orchestrated everything to look like some show, and the tourists eat it up, thinking it is the best entertainment ever," Peggy responded. "What you see here during your visit is no show. It is our lives. It is our livelihood. I'm afraid we're all at a breaking point."

Paris and Sherlock Holmes exchanged knowing looks once more. Getting to a breaking point sounded like murder was close. They weren't there to stop that, but they were going to solve it.

CHAPTER SIX

Peggy's Pie Shop, Haunted Harbor, Maine, New England, United States

Paris nearly jumped when someone clambered into the shop, she was so on edge from hearing the nightmare happening in Haunted Harbor. The person who entered didn't even notice the group of outsiders at the table. It was a large, bearded man with a head of wiry gray hair. By the looks of the yellow slicker and matching hat he was taking off, he was a fisherman.

Putting his head down, the man shook his head out over the floor mat as if he was accustomed to doing such things. "Oh look, a new floor mat. Nice, Peg. You keep updating things, making them nice."

He shook his head again to clear out all the water in his hair and beard, still bowed over, not realizing anyone else was there. "I swear, those fish must quiver when they hear my name." He chuckled in a deep voice. "I sure would, you know what I mean, Peg?"

The woman didn't answer, watching as the man straightened and hung up his jacket and hat. Finally, he turned and halted, confused at the unfamiliar faces at the table. Finding Peggy's face, the man shot her a perplexed look. "Did Saul endorse you today? I didn't think the tour boat had come in yet?"

Peggy simply shot him a pursed expression.

The man ducked down, looking through the window to the side. "Have the Howell's had overnight visitors, and I missed it? Did these guys stay there last night?"

Peggy shook her head.

Scratching his beard, the burly man appeared at a loss. "Someone's going to have to explain what's going on because I'm out of ideas."

Peggy held out her hand to the group. "This is a group of investigators who found some problems here. They are apparently here to help us. I'm trying to explain to them our situation so they know where to start."

The guy laughed loudly, a nice sound full of spirit. "Where to start? Over would be my best bet. I tell you, we should just burn this whole place down and start again."

Peggy waved her hand dismissively at him. "Oh, you can say that because you've got your boat and the water and nothing here on land."

He grinned at her. "I'm on land right now and looking for a piece of my pie, but I don't see that."

Peggy slid out of the booth. "Oh, fine, Barry. I'll go get your pie."

"What kind is it?" King Rudolf asked.

"Berry. It's the best pie they have here," the man answered, striding over and grabbing a chair from a nearby table. He turned it around and sat in it backward. "You all are?"

"I'm Paris and an agent for FGA." She indicated Rudolf. "This is the king of the fae."

"That one there is Sherlock Holmes," Peggy cut in, striding over and putting a piece of mixed berry pie down in front of Barry. "That's my last slice of that, so don't ask for another."

"Seems like an interesting group," the fisherman said, taking the fork and going straight to work on his pie, the berries coloring his beard from the start. "What is it that you need to know? Besides that we're being ruled over by a tyrant who I fear is cleverer than the rest of us. Lord knows he's always one step ahead of us."

"Aside from owning the tourist industry here," Paris began, "how does Saul affect your businesses and life?"

Peggy slid back into the booth. "He manipulates the tourists. They are fearful from the start when they get here."

Sherlock Holmes nodded. "We heard a portion of that brainwashing from the boat. He said something about how they needed to get outfitted, but even then they had to follow his every word."

Barry shook his head. "Fear is the most powerful motivator. He starts by telling them to mock Rebecca. Then he takes them to Dagger Island, where he sells them vests and crystals and all sorts of other junk supposed to keep them safe from the ghosts. There's nothing here to hurt them. Just lies all told by him."

"That's not the worst of it," Peggy said. "He tells them, depending on his mood, what establishments to patronize during their several hours exploring our town. You'll hear him when he drops them off. We all do because he turns that speaker up so loud, knowing we want to know what to expect for the day, and hoping he endorses our businesses."

"I don't really understand," Paris said, scratching her head and hoping she didn't sound like a dumb blonde. Sherlock Holmes didn't seem to be following either.

"For instance," Peggy continued. "Most days, he tells the tourists that my pies have been cursed by the ghosts and only the locals can eat them without getting sick."

"Oh, so when they see Barry in here, they think he's okay because he lives here," Rudolf guessed. "They wouldn't dare to venture in, fearful of getting sick."

"That's right," Peggy stated. "Currently, Maureen and Jason, who own the Howell's Inn, have been granted partial leniency. Lately, he tells the tourists that it's the only safe place to eat but that sleeping in Haunted Harbor overnight would result in certain deaths for nonlocals."

Paris sighed heavily. "That's so manipulative. How can one person control so much? Can't you fight back?"

"When we do, we just look like loons," Barry stated. "He's programmed them from the start to not trust us. He even tells them on the boat ride the locals are all crazy from living with ghosts. If we demand he's wrong, they just nod, having been told we'd try to convince them. He goes so far as to say that we want to trick them, so they die here and haunt our town, giving us more company because we're so lonely and can't leave."

"Why don't you leave?" Paris asked, confused why anyone would put up with so much abuse.

"This is our home. I built this shop from the ground up decades ago. Even if I could afford to move on," Peggy said, suddenly sentimental as she looked out at the harbor. "We can't let him win. If Saul Senior knew what his son was doing, he'd make him pay. He didn't come back as a ghost. I sure wish he had."

Barry shook his head. "I've been fishing these waters all my life, the same as my father. I'm not going anywhere. I still fish even if I can't really sell all of them each day."

"Why can't you?" Sherlock Holmes asked.

"Because I'm on the bad list," Barry told him. "Not as bad as Peggy, who is only allowed to make money from locals. Saul needs me. He doesn't like pie."

"Explain," Rudolf demanded. "I have a high IQ, but I don't read between the lines."

Barry sighed. "Back in the day, I sold my fish at the market here, and to the Fish Fry and local restaurants and the tour companies who have lunch cruises. Guess who I'm allowed to sell to now?"

"Only Saul," Paris guessed. "I still don't get it. Just sell it at the market and all."

"That's fine and I do," Barry replied. "Only the locals will buy from them."

Paris understood at once. Her heart hurt for these people. "Saul tells the tourists not to eat at the restaurants, only the Howell's Inn, and not to buy from the market or the Fish Fry."

"Yeah, they'll get deathly ill if they eat the fish in Haunted Harbor and become ghosts," Barry said, pushing away his unfinished pie. "If they eat the fish he offers for the evening meal on his cruise back to the big city port, that's fine. So I sell to him, but I'm forced to sell at half my usual price."

Peggy glanced at the dish offended and swiped it away, putting it on another table.

"Why don't you refuse?" Sherlock Holmes asked the man.

"Because..." Barry shrugged. "I need the money. I sell to the markets and restaurants at regular prices, but they don't buy as much because they can't sell as much."

Peggy shook her head. "Tourism has always been this little town's lifeblood. We are out of the way of the main roads, mostly accessible by boat, and we don't have any exports that set us apart. You think we can sell our fish to other places in New England? They all have their own fish. We had our ghosts, and it brought people from all over. We all profited. We were happy, enjoying making a living, seeing fresh faces, and living on the water. Now we're as good as ghosts ourselves."

When the door opened again, the person who came through noticed the new faces right away. The balding round man in a button-up shirt and slacks paused in the doorway, his mouth falling open and eyes wide.

Peggy laughed. "Mayor Dagger, these are investigators, and they are here to help us fix our town, if at all possible. I know you're surprised, as Barry and I were just momentarily. Go ahead and get in here, and we'll get you up to speed."

CHAPTER SEVEN

Peggy's Pie Shop, Haunted Harbor, Maine, New England, United States

"Y-Yo-You're Sherlock Holmes," Mayor Harrison Dagger stuttered, looking at the great detective.

He nodded. "And we have a lot more questions for you all. For instance, we're going to need to know exactly who all in the town has been at the receiving end of Saul's sabotage and how."

Paris knew exactly why Sherlock Holmes wanted this information. After the murder, whoever it happened to, they would need to find out who had a motive. There was a lot at play in this tiny little fishing village.

"I don't even know where to begin," Mayor Dagger said, pressing his hand to his chest and looking faint.

"How are you feeling, Harrison?" Peggy asked him, looking the man up and down concernedly.

"I'm fine, Peg."

The woman shook her head, glancing back at the others. "Harrison here is sick, and all this stress has just made it worse."

"Don't tell strangers that," Harrison scolded.

"Oh, as if most can't look at you see you're practically on your

145

death bed," she said, shaking her head at him. She looked hurt. "You'll be a ghost in no time at this rate."

"Can I get a cup of coffee?" he asked her.

She shook her head. "I don't think that's good for you. Your heart."

"My heart is fine," Harrison argued. "Can I have some pie?"

"No, it can't be good for you," she said, crossing her arms in front of her chest stubbornly.

"I have to eat and drink, or I will die," he stated, sounding more annoyed now.

"You have that drink every night with that soulless monster," she said through clenched teeth.

"On that note, I better be getting out to my boat. Saul will be coming in soon, and I've got to send over their shipment for the return meal." Barry stood, looking down at the others. "I hope that you all can help us, otherwise, I don't know what will happen to Haunted Harbor."

"We'll try." And it was King Rudolf who said this, but even he didn't appear as hopeful and carefree as usual. This was a strange and complex situation.

The old fisherman left without another word, making the café suddenly quiet as the mayor and Peggy exchanged irritated looks.

"Can you fill us in on what you mean about having a drink with this monster every night?" Sherlock Holmes asked, breaking their stare off.

Harrison sighed, looking at the detective. "I have to. I know that it makes Peggy mad, but it's something I have to do. You see, Saul pretty much owns part of this town now. We'd be a ghost town if he didn't run his tours."

"That's not funny," Peggy admonished.

"It's true, Peg. He's ruined our reputation. He controls the marketing of what people believe about Haunted Harbor. He runs the boat. If I don't do business with him, he's promised to make us sound like a nuclear wasteland that no one will go near.

I don't have the money to campaign against that. He's too far entrenched in all the tourist agencies. They sell his tours. I can't change that."

Peggy shook her head, getting up and heading for the kitchen. This had apparently been an ongoing feud between the two.

"Continue," Paris urged the mayor. "Tell us about these nightly meetings."

"Saul says that whatever money we make, however little, he deserves a cut," Harrison explained. "So each night, after the tour is over and he's returned, we sit down for a drink. I go over that day's revenue and the books for Haunted Harbor. We negotiate, and sometimes I get him to endorse Peggy's business the next day or open the market or something. I'm at his mercy. I hope you see that. I have to give him a cut of what our businesses make, or he'll just make this worse."

"He's the reason people aren't making money," Paris argued. "You can't even have overnight tourism."

Harrison shook his head. "No, he's worried he would lose control if people stayed for too long. He controls every aspect of the town."

"Why do you meet every night?" Sherlock Holmes asked. "Why not once a week?"

"All of this was a shock in the beginning," Harrison began. "I was hoping that I could change things if I intervened. It became evident early on that wasn't going to happen. Still, I gunned for daily meetings, hoping I could argue until he was tired of it and gave up this horrible dictatorship of his. When he didn't, I tried to save my stress and health and ask to meet less, but then I realized what that sick man was addicted to."

Sherlock Holmes nodded. "He likes watching you all suffer."

Harrison growled in frustration. "He loves watching me beg, knowing I love this place he hates and wanted to leave for so long."

"Sadly, he can leave now, but he sticks around to torture you all," Paris said, shaking her head at the grossness of it.

Harrison nodded. "You'll see in just a minute. Saul loves making us all suffer from morning until night. If I try to cancel with him, he threatens to not bring the tour the next day and to run a marketing campaign to ruin us for good. I can't risk that. Too many are dependent on the little tourism that we get."

King Rudolf pointed out the window. "It appears the pirate is here. Shall we go and pay him a visit?"

"I'd caution you to stay out of sight," Harrison said, suddenly sweating as he watched the large pirate ship glide into the harbor. "I'll take you around town and show you what I can. You can watch Saul's speech from the shadows. I fear that whatever investigation you're conducting will be over the moment he finds out you're here. He'll load up the boat of tourists and not come back, ever."

Paris glanced at Sherlock, who nodded minutely. She wanted to go and punch the bully controlling every aspect of this town. She reminded herself their job was to get the water for the antidote, solve a murder, and then fix the town. That meant playing this just right.

She forced a smile. "We'd love a tour, Mayor Dagger."

CHAPTER EIGHT

Haunted Harbor, Maine, New England, United States

Mayor Harrison Dagger was able to covertly lead the three outsiders around the back of the shops and to a dark alleyway where they had a perfect view of the pirate ship when it docked. Once in place, the crew jumped down and expertly went to work tying up the boat into place.

The Haunted Harbor Pirate Tour was brimming with eager visitors excited to stroll through the town full of ghosts. They were all wearing black vests like the crew but emblazoned with logos and crests that said things like, "Protected." Many had large crystals hanging around their necks. Some wore ballcaps that read: Under the Protection of Salty Saul. All of them appeared ready to race through the streets and find a ghost.

Even for Paris it seemed like an intriguing idea, and she kept looking around for an apparition. Crammed in the dark alleyway with three men, she didn't see much. Thankfully, she was at the front and had a view of the ship.

When Captain Salty Saul took his place at the entrance to the dock leading to Main Street, she could see details of the evil pirate wannabe. The man was short and appeared like a large gnome in his pirate outfit. When he took off his hat, Paris noticed he had short spiky brown hair with a gray streak through it. Most annoying was the evil glint in his eyes.

He raised his hands overhead, facing the crowd on the boat. With the microphone in one hand, he pressed it to his mouth. "You are about to set off on a chilly ghost hunting adventure. You have one hour, and if you don't return I'll assume that you've been turned into one and will be a part of the next tour."

The crowd laughed. Paris didn't.

"Now, as your captain, what do you call me?" Saul asked.

"Captain Salty Saul," the visitors sang in unison from the boat.

"Yes! You can also call me by two other esses," he continued, his speech obviously rehearsed. "You can call me Captain Safety Saul for as long as I'm close by, you'll have no real worries of becoming a ghost. All you have to do is use the app you purchased on Dagger Island from my company to alert me that you need help. If a local approaches you in any way that makes you feel uncomfortable, use the app. If one of them pressures you, alert me. Know these people have been living with the ghosts for a long time and they are crazy." He made the motion beside his head for "crazy" and the crowd all laughed. Again, Paris didn't, not amused by this inhumane abuse of power.

"You shouldn't fear the ghosts, for the most part," Salty Saul went on. "If for any reason you feel uncomfortable based on what I've told you, then use the app. Yes, each message will cost you, but isn't your safety worth that?"

"Yes," the tourists all answered.

Paris couldn't believe how much this man had monetized this exploit. She considered she might kill him, and then there would be no mystery of who did anything. She was starting to understand why the animosity was so high here. Haunted Harbor had been infected by a disease, and it was Salty Saul.

"Now," the fake captain continued, "you can also call me Captain Smart Saul. I'm here for you and know everything there is to know about this haunted town. That means what I tell you, pay attention to. If you do what I say, you'll leave here alive. If you disobey, then you will stay here as a ghost."

"Wow, this guy is good," Paris whispered to Sherlock and Rudolf beside her.

They both agreed.

"Today it appears that Howell's Inn is the only safe place to grab a snack," Saul said, which was met with many groans from the crowd.

He held up his hands. "No worry, my fellow ghost hunters. I'll feed you a hearty fish supper on your voyage home." Salty Saul pointed to the other side of the dock where Barry the fisherman was doing the hard work of hauling his cargo from his morning work to the large ship. "The local fisherman has us stocked with fish that we will prepare in a very special way to ensure that you don't catch the ghost virus that sometimes permeates the food in this here harbor. Once it's on board the Haunted Harbor Pirates Tour, it will be safe for your consumption once you pay the meal fee."

This was met with applause. Paris couldn't believe how much manipulation this man was responsible for.

"Now, to keep you safe," Captain Salty Saul continued. "You're to stay away from the markets, gift shops, eateries, and especially you're not allowed to stay overnight. That means meet me back here in one hour. Oh, and if you see the Witch of the Ghosts, you remember what to do, right?"

In unison, the crowd began singing, "Puff the magic dragon lived by the sea."

Salty Saul grinned wide and clapped his hands. "You're the best ghost hunters I've had in a long time. Now with that, happy hunting."

The crew opened the gates and the visitors all spilled onto the docks and into the streets of Haunted Harbor. They'd search for ghosts, leave trash, and disrupt the village, but not help the people living there.

Paris simply had to fix this place. And she would.

CHAPTER NINE

Haunted Harbor, Maine, New England, United States

The group waited until the tourists had moved off down the main street and Captain Salty Saul had gone the opposite direction. According to Mayor Dagger, the pirate took turns harassing different residents depending on his mood. On this occasion, it appeared he was headed down to Peggy's Pie Shop Paris saw when she ducked out of the alleyway.

Harrison waved them the opposite way up the alley, more inland. "We'll go this way, and I'll show you some of the streets that will be off limits to the visitors and therefore safe for us to walk."

The group walked one way and then another for a long time, mostly just taking a tour of the village in silence.

"Your last name is Dagger," Sherlock Holmes said after a long time to the mayor as they had walked. "The tour stopped off on Dagger Island. Is that any relation to you?"

He nodded. "It's named after my family, the Daggers. My great-great-grandfather founded Haunted Harbor. He was an explorer and came here and met a ghost. He wasn't afraid and built a house and started the small village. Over time, he realized that some who died here became ghosts, although the scientific or cosmic reasons are still unclear. It's not exact anyway. Not everyone becomes a ghost who lives and dies here. Not all ghosts stick around. Definitely nothing that Saul says about people breaking the rules turns them into ghosts."

"It's because there's a window here that bleeds into the land of the dead," King Rudolf said quite seriously.

Everyone paused and looked back at the fae.

"Are you sure?" Sherlock Holmes asked.

He nodded. "Yes, think about it. There are places in the world where ours bleeds into others. This just happens to be one where the walls between the land of the living and the dead are very thin. That means seeing into the land of the dead isn't as difficult as in other areas. Really, ghosts are everywhere in other places, but they are in the land of the dead. Here, we share a bathroom, if you will, so you bump into them all the time. Think of it like you're sharing a hostel with the dead. It's not that weird."

Sherlock Holmes gave Paris a sideways look. "That makes perfect sense."

"Isn't he amazing like that?" she said, smiling at her strange uncle.

Both of the other men nodded.

"So your family founded Haunted Harbor," King Rudolf said, ushering the group to continue walking, strangely taking charge.

The mayor nodded. "Yes, and we've been here ever since. I like your explanation, and it makes sense but still this is a strange place. Those who live here wouldn't live anywhere else, as you've seen. And then it is a wonderful place for those who want to see ghosts but in a safe way. We've never had a problem."

"Because ghosts can't hurt you," Rudolf related, again a wealth of information. "They literally can't, with no way to affect the living. Most of the time, they don't even know we're around. They are living in their own worlds. Again quite literally. But many are afraid of what they don't understand. Now poltergeists are another story."

"That's in line with what I know," Mayor Dagger said with a nod. "There's an island just south of here that's not haunted and full of beauty and vegetation. Saul always starts his tours there so he can upsell people and go over the rules before the final speech. That's where my grandfather initially started before he found the harbor."

"It's a beautiful place," Paris offered. "We'll do everything we can to help you save it. We need to know as much as you can tell us about the people. That's key."

"Also, what the hell is that?" King Rudolf had halted by a shop on the cobbled street and was pointing to a strange sign that read: Ghost Repair Shop.

CHAPTER TEN

Haunted Harbor, Maine, New England, United States

Mayor Harrison Dagger glanced up at the shop sign and chuckled, covering his mouth. "Oh, that. Since we're kind of a different place, we have some different kinds of shops to fit our needs."

"Ghost repair shop," Paris read, studying the front window. It didn't appear out of the ordinary, although there were some strange instruments and a few objects she didn't recognize.

"Yeah, we love our ghosts," Harrison explained. "We have quite a few that have been with us for a long time. Sometimes they begin to flicker, and we worry they are leaving us. Or they get sad and have problems. There are many residents who have their own family ghosts, but they might have problems with them where they start making noises at night or waking them up talking. Anyway, people visit the ghost repair shop for help or answers. It's all very experimental, and really it only works half the time."

"Because you can't fix ghosts," King Rudolf said, shaking his head as if this was obvious. "They are people. They're not devices. Their problems have to be approached the same way that you would with a person alive. They will fade at times, but they can come back depending on their activity. They'll make noise if they are restless or going through things. You can try talking to them and helping them. But if they aren't aware of your existence, well, then there's not much you can do. Sounds like you're trying to fix metaphysical problems with technology." He laughed. "That's like trying to fix a philosophical problem with a wrench. Do you really think that will work?"

Harrison thought about this. "Can we contract you as a consultant?"

Rudolf shook his head and threw up his hands. "I don't know the first thing about ghosts. I think if you start to think of them as being there and not really being there, you'll get all this better. Stop trying to keep them or make them do something. You'd never do that with actual people. Not unless you're my wife. Just let them be and realize that you share a communal wall and there are big holes in it. Like giant holes. Enjoy them. Pass notes back and forth. Knock on the walls. Make games. Know that sometimes they won't knock back, and sometimes they'll knock all the time. There's no repairing ghosts."

Harrison drew in a breath and smiled. "I think this has been one of the best and most enlightening days I've had in months."

Paris grinned at her uncle. "King Rudolf has a way of doing that."

"He does," Sherlock Holmes said, setting off again. "Now, tell us about Rebecca Flores. She seems like an important character who Saul enjoys torturing."

Harrison hung his head. "Oh, that's a heartbreaker. You see, Rebecca and Saul were once engaged to be married. She didn't love him, so she broke it off and married another man. A wonderful one. Mr. Jonathon Flores. They married and moved to the house you see on the island there." He indicated the direction where Paris had seen the beautiful woman.

"Last year, Jonathon was found dead," Harrison continued. "It was Rebecca who found him on their lawn. It was after a big party, and the music was still playing. Most of us were inside the house, but when we rushed out, she was in shock. Playing was—"

"Puff the Magic Dragon," Paris guessed.

He nodded.

"That's so cruel," Paris said. "So Saul tortures her by making her into this villain for the tours. Then he makes them sing the song that reminds her of her husband's death. He has them mock her."

Harrison shook his head. "Saul isn't right in the head."

A strange bass noise sounded in the distance, pausing everyone. They all looked around trying to find the source of the music. It was indistinguishable except for gentle beats.

"What's that?" Paris asked the mayor.

"I'm not sure," he answered. "Probably the boat and the excited tourists."

"Have we been walking for an hour?" Paris asked, wondering if time moved differently there.

"Probably close," Harrison answered. "Anyway, as I was saying, Saul is dangerous and cruel. I believe he murdered Jonathon. Just like with everything else he's done, there's no way to prove anything. I've tried. I've gone to the authorities, and they say he's running a business. They don't take us seriously, thinking we're all kooky."

"Probably because he's slandered your character," Paris reasoned. "He uses every advantage to make you look untrustworthy and dangerous to outsiders."

Harrison might have been about to agree, but his phone rang, and he excused himself momentarily.

Paris turned to the other two men. Rudolf regarded his hand like it was of unique interest. Sherlock was looking up at the hills. Here they weren't dotted with houses but rather wild vegetation of various colors.

"It looks like we'll have our work cut out for us," Paris said. "How much longer do you think we'll have here?"

"I'm not sure," Rudolf said, not taking his eyes off his hand.

Before Sherlock Holmes could reply, Harrison shut off his phone with a strange look.

"What is it?" Paris asked.

"That was Saul," he said, obviously confused.

"Oh, does he know about us? Are you in trouble?" Paris questioned.

The mayor shook his head. "I don't think so. He canceled our evening meeting. He said he had an offer he couldn't turn down." Finally bringing his dazed eyes up, Harrison suddenly looked worried. "Salty Saul said Rebecca begged him to have a drink with her tonight."

Sherlock Holmes cut his eyes to Paris. "To answer your previous question, it won't be long *now*."

CHAPTER ELEVEN

Haunted Harbor, Maine, New England, United States

Because they were so far north and it was summer, the sun didn't set as early as Paris was used to. So when she caught the rays of light well past usual, she was surprised by how late it was.

The glistening light across the harbor was beautiful even if Paris knew this place was suffering. The strange beat they'd heard earlier had gone off once but then not again. Now it was quiet in the shadows of the alleyway where King Rudolf, Sherlock Holmes and Paris were waiting. For what she didn't know.

Mayor Dagger had left them, saying he was going to use this time to catch up on business. The man was on edge, sweating profusely, but Paris thought she would be in his situation too.

The tourists were all gone and had been for the better part of two hours. Paris and her friends were growing weary of waiting. Again, she wasn't sure for what. A murder, yes, but when and who and where. It was like a mystery inside of a mystery.

King Rudolf was leaning against the brick wall, continuing to stare at his hand like earlier. Sherlock Holmes was at the far side of the alleyway that led inland where they walked earlier, studying something up high. Paris was perched by the corner of the alleyway that faced out to the harbor. That's why she noticed the pirate ship when it sailed back to the dock like before.

Standing on the bow of the large, shiny ship was the small man, Captain Salty Saul.

"Hey, he's coming back," Paris called to the others, waving them to come see.

They both trotted over and looked as the ship steered up to the dock. The crew was along the rails, ready to jump down and secure the vessel into place for the night. Their captain didn't look right. He was swaying, then he was staggering. His crew didn't notice, too preoccupied with their jobs.

When Captain Salty Saul dove forward, losing all control, no one but the three paying close attention saw what had happened. The evil man fell over the side of the ship and into the harbor with a splash, sinking fast and disappearing at once.

Rudolf glanced at Paris and Sherlock Holmes, his eyes wide. "He's fallen in and looks drunk. Should we save him before he drowns?"

Paris was about to say no.

It was Sherlock who answered, shaking his head. "He's already dead. He's been dead since the moment we arrived, or at least everything was in place for it from then. There's no stopping this."

"Do you know who did this?" Paris asked, surprised since there were so many would-be suspects.

"Yes," Sherlock Holmes said as one of the crew members noticed their captain was floating face down in the water. He yelled to the others, but none looked like they were making any fast movement to retrieve the body.

"Who?" Paris and Rudolf asked at the same time.

"Give me fifteen minutes to check that I'm correct," Sherlock Holmes stated, looking at Rudolf. "Round up Barry, Peggy, Rebecca, and Harrison and meet us at the pie shop."

"The main suspects," Paris guessed.

The great detective nodded. "I think you know what you have to do?"

Paris glanced at the choppy waters of the harbor where the crew were making a slow effort to get the dead body out. "Retrieve the water for the antidote."

"That's one of the main reasons we came here," Sherlock Holmes said.

"The other one?" Paris asked, hopefully.

He smiled at her, and then his gaze drifted to where the crew was dragging the dead man's body from the harbor. "This place will be better when we leave. It's already better. Soon these people will have closure. Now be off."

CHAPTER TWELVE

Peggy's Pie Shop, Haunted Harbor, Maine, New England, United States

The water from the harbor sloshed in the potion bottles in Paris' jacket when she strode into Peggy's Pie Shop fifteen minutes later. News spread fast about Captain Salty Saul's death, which had been confirmed. Paris had checked his pulse herself. He was gone. Although they would do an autopsy to confirm the cause of death, she was certain that if the great detective said he already knew who did it, that was true.

The air in the café was thick with tension when Paris entered to find the residents King Rudolf had been ordered to collect.

"You said you'd come here to investigate," Peggy said in a shrill voice. "What did that mean?"

"It meant exactly that," Paris replied, standing in front of the door as all the suspects stood as if planning to make a break for it.

King Rudolf stepped in front of her, pressing his hands down. "If you can just take a seat, we're going to get to the bottom of things. You can rest assured the monster is gone, and your town will return to you soon."

"I didn't murder him," Peggy said, striding back and forth in her apron.

"Neither did I," Barry said at once.

"Why are we even talking about that?" the woman who was Rebecca Flores asked. She was even more beautiful up close with her ruby red lips and flowing brown hair.

"Because Sherlock Holmes is here," Barry said. "They must have known there would be a murder."

"We knew there was a problem here," Paris stated.

"You really came to fix it?" Mayor Harrison Dagger asked.

Paris gave him a sensitive expression, moving further into the dining area. "I'm an agent for FGA. My job is to ensure that love on all levels is maintained and nurtured. And it was obviously at stake here. Yes, I work with Sherlock Holmes and King Rudolf, but that's just coincidental. But yes, there's been a murder. And we have to solve it. Then we put this town back together, and you all go back to living your lives, hopefully better than before, knowing what you lost."

At the conclusion of her words, Sherlock Holmes entered the café, a stoic expression on his face. He looked at the four people stationed in different places in the large room. He swallowed. Tilted his head to the side. Withdrew his unlit pipe from his jacket pocket.

"I know who murdered Captain Salty Saul," he began in a clear voice, standing squarely in front of the door and the exit, as it were. "If that person wants to step forward, then we can save some time. If not, then I'll give my full report."

Paris glanced around at the various suspects—Peggy, Barry, Harrison, and Rebecca. They looked at each other as though expecting one of them to shout, "It was me."

When no one did, Sherlock Holmes nodded as if he'd expected this. "Very well. Everyone take a seat, and I'll run through the events exactly as I believe they happened today and in the past, leading to the death of a man. Yes, a bad one, but a death regardless. And then I'll reveal who I think the killer is…"

CHAPTER THIRTEEN

Peggy's Pie Shop, Haunted Harbor, Maine, New England, United States
The death of the man who had ruined their lives hadn't reunited the residents of Haunted Harbor. At least not yet. Each took a seat at opposite corners of the café. Paris and King Rudolf sat together in the booth where they'd dined earlier that day. It was hard to believe it was the same day, feeling like so much time had passed. Paris was grateful Mother Nature had given her an extra dose of energy or whatever it was that she gave her to keep her going.

Sherlock Holmes waited until everyone was in place, then started pacing in the aisle between tables, holding his pipe in his mouth as he studied the floor.

"A person who had suffered greatly under Saul's rule is the person's shop where we reside now."

"It wasn't me," Peggy exclaimed. "I didn't kill him."

"He did come by this afternoon, prior to his death," Sherlock Holmes stated rather definitively.

"Well, yes," Peggy replied, her tone shaking.

"And what happened?" Sherlock Holmes asked.

"I thought you said you knew who killed him?" Peggy asked. "Why are you questioning if you know? Just come out with it."

Sherlock Holmes paused. "A good detective doesn't simply make accusations. I have a very strong hunch, let's call it. But to know that it is actually the right indictment, I must first question each of you. Please bear with me. I know you've been through a lot."

Peggy nodded. Made to smile. "Very well. I don't have anything to hide. That's fair." She drew in a breath and then seemed to hold back tears. "Saul did come by earlier while the visitors were exploring our town. He demanded a piece of pie, but I told him I didn't have any for him." She laughed, but it made her nearly burst into tears again. "I told him I'd name a pie after him called Saul Seaweed."

This actually made the other's laugh.

Peggy shook her head, pushing at her eyes. "Anyway, he made me serve him. Said that this week he'd allow visitors to patronize my shop if I complied." She shook her head. "It was always just a power play with him. He just wants what he wants and uses what he has to get it, knowing he has control. Yes, I gave him a piece of pie."

"Which pie?" Sherlock Holmes asked calmly.

She drew in a breath, seeming surprised by the question. "Well, it was late, so what we had left. Does it really matter?"

"It always matters in these events."

She pointed to the cases of pies in the back. "It was Peggy's Pecan." And a moment later, she added, "But I didn't kill him. There's no poison here if that's what you're insinuating."

"I'm not," Sherlock Holmes told her. "I simply wanted to know what was in his system at the time of death."

"The coroner will tell us that," Barry offered.

"True," Sherlock Holmes stated. "But they are mortals, and may not be as well versed in some of the more complex things that might be at play here."

"What does that mean?" Barry asked.

"You served the fish that was Saul's dinner tonight, is that correct?" Sherlock Holmes asked the fisherman.

"Well, of course I did. I always do. He makes me," the man answered.

"But today you were extra bitter," Sherlock stated. "Why was that?"

"Extra?" Barry asked. "I don't know what you mean."

"You didn't eat all your pie," Sherlock Holmes recalled.

"I don't see why that's relevant."

"Well, you usually do," Sherlock Holmes stated.

"How would you know that?"

"Because of what Peggy said when she served it about not asking for another," Sherlock answered. "And because of her look of offense when you didn't eat it all."

Barry shook his head. "Fine, I was extra bitter. Is that what you want to hear?"

"I don't relish in your pain," Sherlock Holmes answered. "It's just that you were upset, more so than usual, which could be a cause to put poison in someone's fish who is the cause of your grief."

"I didn't kill Saul," Barry barked.

Sherlock Holmes started pacing.

"Look, if you think that Peggy or me killed Saul, just say it. I want to know what evidence you have!"

Sherlock Holmes paused. "I don't think either of you did. Peggy doesn't have a motive. And you don't have it in you."

"What?" Rebecca and Harrison asked in unison.

"But Saul was ruining Peggy's business," Barry argued.

"He was trying," Sherlock said. "She's smart, so she tried her hand at something else. Didn't you?" He flickered his gaze to the baker.

She blushed and looked at the floor. "How did you know?"

"The new floor mat," Sherlock told her. "The new furnishings. You've come into money."

"I don't see how you could conclude that," she said, not making eye contact.

"You were out of the most loved pie, Barry's Berries," Sherlock Holmes continued. "Only locals can dine here, and I've done the math. You shouldn't be sold out unless you're able to sell somewhere else."

She looked off. "I know a cargo route and have been shipping some pies out. I found a distributor. They love the Barry's Berries."

"That's great, Peg," Harrison said, looking happy for his friend.

"Yes, thank you."

"You said it wasn't me," Barry said, bringing it back to him.

"I said you didn't have it in you," Sherlock Holmes corrected. "No, it wasn't you. You've been serving Saul's fish dinner for months. It would be very easy to serve him a bad fish. You haven't because of what you said earlier. Fishing is in your blood. You'll do it even if you don't get paid. You'll do it even if you can't sell your fish. There's no way you'd ever put your reputation, or your family's on the line by serving bad fish, even if it killed a bad man."

The group fell silent.

Rebecca stood up suddenly, her lip quivering. "I guess you all think it was me then, because I asked Saul to join me for a drink tonight."

"Why do you come out to the pier when the tour boat goes by?" Sherlock Holmes asked, not losing his cool.

"Be-Be-Because Saul can always make things harsher," Rebecca answered. "He made threats. Said he'd find other ways to make my life even worse. I didn't know what that was, but I decided to just do it instead of fretting over how he could hurt me. I mean, he already killed my husband. The man scared me."

"You decided you were done with the humiliation, didn't you?" Sherlock Holmes asked. "You decided that you'd beat him at his own game."

"What do you mean?" Peggy asked.

"Saul tried to hurt Rebecca with the song that played at the time she found her husband dead," he answered. "Making her relive it over and over again." Sherlock clicked his tongue, shaking his head before turning his full attention to Rebecca. "What did you decide to do about it?"

She shook her head. "How do you know about that?"

He pointed to his ear. "I was classically trained in music."

"What is he talking about?" Harrison asked.

Tears flowed down Rebecca's cheeks. "I was tired of him humiliating me and making me listen to that song. So I decided to beat him at his own game. To take the fun out of it for him. I had speakers installed all over my property. When he came over for the drink I invited him for, after the cruise, I played Puff the Magic Dragon. I stood there and played it and had a drink, and then I played it again and showed him that I didn't care. That I'd play it over and over again. I knew it took the enjoyment out of it for him."

Rudolf applauded. "Smart. That's how you defeat your enemy."

Sherlock Holmes nodded. "I heard it and knew the tune, even from just the bass."

"Impressive," Paris offered. "So Rebecca didn't poison him with a drink?"

Sherlock Holmes shook his head. "No, the person that killed Captain Salty Saul wasn't the one who fed him pie tonight." He nodded at Peggy. "It wasn't the one who fed him dinner." He pointed to Barry. "It most definitely wasn't the person who gave him a drink." He indicated Rebecca.

Turning, the great detective faced the mayor of Haunted Harbor. "Ironically, the person who killed that awful man was the one who didn't serve him anything. That's exactly what killed him."

CHAPTER FOURTEEN

Peggy's Pie Shop, Haunted Harbor, Maine, New England, United States

"Say what?" King Rudolf asked, shaking his head.

Sherlock Holmes chewed on his pipe contemplatively before putting it back in his pocket and glancing at Mayor Harrison Dagger. "You are a very smart man. A loyal leader. And someone who plans."

"I don't know if I should be thanking you for that compliment," Harrison said, mopping his sweating brow.

"You knew from the beginning that Saul wouldn't stop," Sherlock began. "So you decided then how you could get rid of him. That's why you started the nightly meetings, which were accompanied by a drink."

"He made me," Harrison argued.

"At first, you insisted," Sherlock stated. "And you, knowing what he wanted, begged and pleaded in those meetings, realizing he'd want them to continue to feed his ego."

"I was trying to get my town back."

"I realize that," Sherlock consoled. "But then you tried to back off the meetings."

"They were dehumanizing," Harrison argued.

"Their ending would also be Saul's, as you had planned."

"I don't know what you're talking about!"

"What are you talking about?" Paris asked, needing to understand.

Sherlock Holmes turned to face Paris. "Harrison knows this area better than anyone. He knows that it is home to a very rare plant that's also strangely poisonous."

"You poisoned Saul?" Peggy asked.

Harrison shook his head.

Sherlock did too. "No, he reverse poisoned him." From his pocket, the great detective pulled out a purple weed. Paris recognized it as one of the plants on the hill above where they had walked. "This is a rosenid. A very strange plant that only those who have a lot of experience with could use properly. They might even need centuries of experience. Or maybe just information from elders who have passed."

There was a collective gasp in the room as everyone understood the implication of what Sherlock Holmes was saying.

"The way rosenid works," the detective continued, "is it doesn't poison. Instead, you lace it into someone's drink or food every single day, slowly building up the potency. It doesn't taste or smell. Then, as an unperceived drug, the body becomes dependent on it. If one day, for instance on a day like today, the person drugged doesn't get their dose of rosenid, which would be quite high by now, after all these months, then they would die roughly within hours. Much faster if it was paired with something like nuts, which makes the effects stronger."

"Oh wow," Peggy said, covering her mouth. "I had no idea."

"No, you didn't," Sherlock Holmes agreed. "There's no way you could because your mayor was willing to do this all alone. He'd sacrifice everything for his town." He turned to face Harrison. "I realize you thought you could get rid of Saul in the first month, but he made you continue to meet with him, and so you did, torturing yourself, hoping one day to skip a meeting. But it wasn't until today that it happened. That you got your chance. Because you could never have done it by simply not giving him the drug because that would put you at the scene of the crime. You were always hoping for a day when Saul simply didn't want the meeting. Then he'd be elsewhere and die mysteriously."

"I never wanted this," Harrison moaned. "I tried to reason with him. To negotiate. He was too powerful."

"What you did was murder. But why you did it, was for noble reasons, to free people you love. I can't condone it, but…for a dying man, I might be able to overlook it."

Paris couldn't believe it. But she also knew that imprisoning a man who probably wouldn't live much longer would serve no purpose. And that Haunted Harbor deserved their leader, one who was willing to do everything to help them, even if it killed him.

"Thank you." It was Rebecca who spoke first, standing up and striding over, hugging Harrison.

This was followed by Peggy and then Barry. It was strange to see a person who had done a bad deed rewarded, but it reminded Paris of her ultimate mission. There was good and bad in the world. Not just gray and nihilism. And she had to fix that. Thankfully she had what she needed to do so. The second part of the antidote.

Feeling tired, she realized that she needed to move on to that task before the magic reserves from Amantis quit containing nihil.

Standing, Paris waved Sherlock and Rudolf for the door. "We have to go."

"You're leaving?" Harrison asked, pulling away from the group hugging him.

Paris nodded. "We were just stopping off here. I have another place to save, which is much like this one, and in need of help. And immediately."

"Well, thank you," Harrison said, stepping forward. "I don't know how to thank you actually. I can't even begin to tell you what we've been through and what this will mean to us."

"It's okay. You don't..." Paris trailed away as a white figure stepped through the wall at the back. She widened her eyes at the sight of the ghost, all life like and opaque. Then another figure stepped forward, and another and another and another. Until the entire area around the café was filled with ghosts, all looking at Paris, Sherlock Holmes, and King Rudolf with true gratitude.

"Thank you," the ghosts said in a collective voice.

"Thank you," the residents said. And then in unison they all waved, offering the saviors of Haunted Harbor a true farewell.

MURDER AT THE THEATER

King Rudolf Sweetwater – The handsome and charming king of the fae. He has more money than anyone could possibly spend in ten lifetimes and less braincells than was humanly possible. And yet, his keen instincts and flippant nature made him the perfect assistant to Sherlock Holmes.

Paris Beaufont – As the Director of Advanced Love at Fairy Godmother Agency, the halfling managed high level cases worldwide. Both fairy and magician, with a dose of demon blood, she was smart, sensitive and fierce.

Sherlock Holmes – The great detective's only joy was in solving mysteries. He lacked humor, fake pleasantries or a tolerance for injustice. Under his tough exterior, he cared more for humanity than any other.

Faraday – Once a scientist, a scholar and a man. Presently and for the rest of his life, the genius was stuck as a squirrel. He regretted nothing and was content with being the sidekick to Paris, although he teased that they were, in fact, partners.

William Evermore – Handsome, dashing and desired by many single females. He always plays the lead in the performances at Agatha Theater. Many believe that he's the only thing keeping the doors to the playhouse open. Others say he's the reason that the doors will soon be closing.

Monica Stagecoach – Actress in many of the plays at Agatha Theater. She doesn't stay for the part, but rather to cozy up to the playhouse's star actor.

Phillip O'Hara – Wealthy business owner and patron of the arts in the West End of London. He owns many of the playhouses and has very strict ideas about the future of the district.

Violet Clementine – Stagehand and concession employee for Agatha Theater. It's no secret that she harbors feelings for Charles Kingman. Although she has no ambition herself, she'd love to see him starring in a murder mystery at the theater where she works.

Collette Billings – The Owner of Agatha Theater and Director for all murder mysteries performed there. She inherited the theater from her grandfather and her love of mysteries from his daughter, her mother. Although the theater has fell on harder and harder times, she's unwilling to sell or take on any partners.

Charles Kingman – Usher at Agatha Theater and a budding actor. Although he keeps getting passed over for the lead parts, he hasn't given up hope. Acting is his true passion. It is all that he loves in life.

ACT ONE: THE MEET UP

CHAPTER ONE

Scene One – *Lobby, Agatha Theater, London, United Kingdom*

Most patrons who visited Agatha Theater in London, hoped for a murder mystery, but on this particular night, the audience would witness a real one inside the playhouse.

The old Victorian theater sat in the heart of the West End in London. The spot of Agatha Theater was considered very desirable to most in the district. And yet, even the central location didn't ensure that the shows sold out most nights. If anything, the location had made it the focal point of much controversy.

Many of the surrounding playhouses, spread nasty rumors about Agatha Theater, its actors and most importantly, its owner and director. The local play critics were often giving the performances bad reviews.

Some said it was because the small theater was haunted. Others speculated that it was because the director refused to expand their offerings, only performing murder mystery plays. Many thought that the regular cast of actors were inexperienced or had inflated egos.

But most chalked up the assorted reputation of Agatha

Theater to the fierce competition of the surrounding playhouses. When in business in the West End, it was all about who you knew, how deep your pockets were and how far you were willing to go to get what you wanted.

The lobby of Agatha Theater was elegant and impressive, but undoubtedly worn in places. It was obvious to most who passed through the lobby from the box office to the auditorium, that it had seen better days. Still, the crystal chandeliers hanging overhead usually drew patron's eyes up in awe while their feet remained planted on the red carpet below.

"At the rise of the curtain, it is a brisk autumnal night," King Rudolf Sweetwater began as he and his friends entered the lobby of Agatha Theater. "Rudolf, Paris and Sherlock are seen striding into the rundown playhouse. Paris is wearing a blue evening dress and warm cashmere coat. Sherlock and Rudolf are dressed sharply in tuxedos with top hats."

Paris paused, lowered her chin and regarded the fae with her usual, "I'm going to murder you" expression. "Uncle Rudolf, why are you talking like that?"

"We're seeing a play tonight," he answered, smoothing his white gloved hand over his light-colored hair, not a strand out of place. "I figured I'd spice things up by talking with stage directions, like I'm narrating a playbook. Brilliant idea, am I right?"

She shook her head, her blonde, loose hair windswept from their brisk walk to the playhouse. "It's the worst. And if you keep that up, I will kill you."

"With a candlestick holder?" he asked, arching a curious eyebrow at her.

Paris nodded. "In the drawing room."

He shrugged. "Well, I simply won't go in there. Beat that."

Ignoring her pseudo uncle, which she did often, Paris sighed. "Do you hear that?"

"Do you mean, the sounds proceeding a theatrical performance?" Sherlock Holmes asked, looking handsome but out of place since he wasn't in his usual tweed suit and flat cap.

"Do you mean, the sounds of the general public milling about, brushing up too close to us?" King Rudolf asked, glaring around at all the people gathered in the theater lobby.

Paris shook her head. "No, it's the sound of a day off. No cell phone ringing. No employees and agents whining about their cases. No fires raging that I must put out."

Rudolf cut his eyes at Sherlock. "Poor girl. She really has been working too hard lately. But that's why I recommended a night at the theater. It's good for your spirit, your backside and refilling the creative vault with art and culture. But it also does a number on my liver."

"Why would today make you drink anymore than any other day?" Sherlock Holmes asked, sounding slightly amused.

The detective didn't tolerate most people very well, keeping to himself—living a quiet life…well when he wasn't surrounded by murder. But he had recently decided that King Rudolf made the perfect assistant, replacing Watson. The king's silly nature begged questions that the detective wouldn't have ever thought to ask himself when on a case. And more often than the Londoner wanted to admit, the fae led their investigations in the right direction, either out of pure dumb luck or some unseen brilliance that Sherlock didn't quite fathom.

"Because of all the drama. It makes me drink even more than usual," Rudolf stated, looking around, seemingly searching for something or someone.

Paris laughed. "I think that's part of the charm of the theater. You can't have a show without a villain and a 'who done it' and all the other things that keeps people filing through the doors to see a play."

Rudolf shook his head, tugging the pair in the direction of the bar. "No, I actually mean all the drama that goes along with the theater. It simply drives me to drink, having to be around it." He leaned on the bar, waving for the bartender to come over. "Hey, there, can I get three martinis, please?"

"I don't drink hard liquor," Paris cut in.

The fae scoffed at her. "Those are for me." He turned back to the bartender. "Can I get a glass of your nicest Sauvignon Blanc for my niece and your oldest whiskey for my friend."

"Why thank you," Sherlock Holmes said, sidling up next to them at the bar, having squeezed through the crowd, growing denser.

"Well, I got drinks that reminded me of you both," Rudolf chirped. "Something nice for Paris and something old for you, Sherlock."

Paris took the perspiring glass of white wine the bartender gave her, holding it up to cheers with her companions. "Well, to having a night off and doing something cultured."

"To the theater," Sherlock said, holding up his glass of whiskey.

"To the drama," Rudolf sang, taking his first martini and clinking it against their glasses.

"And to big pockets," Faraday the talking squirrel said, poking his head out of the pouch on the side of Paris' large cashmere coat.

She nearly spilled her drink when the squirrel surprised her, announcing his presence and the obvious fact that he stowed away. "What are you doing in there?"

"Well, I was sleeping and before that, I was having a snack and then I was wondering why you walk like that—"

"Like what?" Paris interrupted, conscious that she was talking to a squirrel in her jacket pocket. Thankfully King Rudolf and Sherlock were surrounding her, all looking down at the rodent.

Faraday shrugged. "You know..."

"I don't," she seethed, distinctly remembering telling her sidekick, the scientist squirrel, that he couldn't join her at the theater that night.

"Well, you walk all hoppity, bouncing around, making it hard for people to sleep," he stated.

"You're not a people," she replied. "You're a freeloading squirrel who was supposed to stay home."

He held up his paw, like trying to interject. "I believe we said that it would be a scene if I was noticed at a posh event like the theater."

"Yes," Paris said, drawing out the word.

"So I just decided that if I wasn't seen, then I could watch the play and we could both have a nice and relaxing time," he stated matter-of-factly.

"But I have a squirrel who stowed away in my pocket and therefore I can't check my coat," Paris stated. "So how relaxed do you think my night is going?"

"Good…" Faraday said, nervousness in his voice.

Before Paris could really lay into the squirrel who was simultaneously the smartest creature she knew and the most annoying, King Rudolf set down his first empty martini glass with a loud clink.

"And so the drama begins…"

Paris jerked her head up, stuffing Faraday down into her pocket. "I'm sorry. I'll make sure that no one sees him. I promise, we won't bring any drama."

King Rudolf shook his head, throwing his head in the direction of a couple making their way over to them, waving at the fae like they knew him. "Not you. And who hasn't seen a squirrel in this theater. I'm pretty sure that there's a huge nest of rats living under the stage." He pretended to smile and then waved back at the couple headed in their direction. "I was referring to the two coming our way. They'll bring drama. I promise you that…"

"Who are they?" Sherlock Holmes asked, leaning over the fae's shoulder.

King Rudolf sighed heavily, looking stressed. "Actors…"

CHAPTER TWO

Scene Two – *Lobby Bar, Agatha Theater, London, United Kingdom*

"Why are they drama?" Faraday asked, his head poking out of Paris' jacket pocket again.

"Why is there a talking animal in my coat?" she said through clenched teeth, shoving him down again.

He replied but she didn't make it out entirely. It sounded like, "I can't see from inside here."

King Rudolf glanced down at the pocket of the coat, like talking to a rodent in a jacket was absolutely normal. "They are drama because she's in love with him. He's in love with himself. And every woman in London is trying to get into his pants while every director is trying to get him to audition for their plays."

"Who is this guy?" Sherlock Holmes asked as the well-dressed man and woman made their way over to King Rudolf.

"The worst human being on the planet," the fae replied and then cut away from his companions and rushed forward, greeting the pair.

He shook the man's hand, pulling him in for a hug. The guy

was mid-twenties, his head full of dark brown hair and not graying at all. He wore a modest suit but was undoubtedly one of those types that would attract the attention of women and directors, as King Rudolf had said. He was boyishly handsome, making it so he could play many parts and also have a wide range of women—both young and older.

"Oh, William, my friend, I swear, not a day goes by I don't think of you," King Rudolf said, cheerfully, patting the man on the back.

The fae pulled away from the man and immediately took the hand of the woman next to him. She was attractive, but not overly so, her features some what masculine. Still, she was thin and wore a small black evening dress that matched her dark long ringlets that hung down her exposed back.

"And Monica, every time I see you, I feel like a better man," the king gushed, kissing the back of her hand.

"Note that this is how he treats people he doesn't like," Sherlock Holmes whispered sideways to Paris.

She nodded. "Noted. And I think because he insults us to our faces, that it means he actually likes us."

"Probably," Faraday said in a hush, having found his way out of the top of the pocket again.

Paris shoved him back down just as the man and woman rounded on them.

"And I'd love for you to meet my niece and goddaughter, Paris Beaufont," King Rudolf said, holding out a presenting hand to her.

She politely smiled, giving her uncle a pointed look. "That's factually untrue. Mom keeps telling you that you're not my godfather."

"Yes, but she also doesn't remember signing those forms either," King Rudolf chimed. "And then also, my lesser-known friend and partner in crime. May I present Sherlock Holmes."

"We solve crimes, not commit them, actually," Sherlock stated. "And he's my assistant, not my partner."

"The Sherlock Holmes?" the man asked. "I can't believe this. I thought you were dead."

"Haven't you heard, darling?" the woman next to him asked, sliding into his arm and laying her hand on his chest. "Sherlock is a mysterious man who has been around for ages and never grows old. No one knows his secrets, but maybe he'll tell us."

"Maybe," the man said, stepping discreetly to the side, away from the woman's attempts at embrace.

"His secret is that he's too boring to die," Rudolf said in a loud whisper. "Believe me, the guy literally does nothing with his time off."

"I'm at the theater," Sherlock spat, sounding slightly offended.

"Why?" Rudolf questioned at once.

The great detective cut his eyes to the side, annoyed. "Because it involves solving a mystery."

"Oh, good one!" the man cheered. "And our play is quite the murder mystery. But firstly, where are my manners. I'm William Evermore. I graduated from Arts Educational School here in London, performed with Royal Shakespeare Company and now I'm the star actor here at Agatha Theater."

"And you are?" Sherlock Holmes asked, narrowing his eyes at the woman who had been pushed to the side by William Evermore.

"Monica Stagecoach," she replied. "I play the lead role opposite of Will. We really have a nice chemistry. That's what many of the papers said yesterday."

"One of them said that," William said, rolling his eyes at her dismissively.

"Well, if one paper said it, then it must be true," Paris said, sensing the obvious tension between the duo.

"I'm a good actor," William gushed, looking toward the bar

and catching his reflection in the mirror of the backsplash and grinning.

King Rudolf picked up his second martini and threw it back. With a sigh, he glared down at Paris. "Do you see what I mean? All drama. All the time."

She nodded, taking a sip of her wine.

"Well, we really better get to hair and makeup," William said, grabbing Monica's hand and holding it up to his mouth and kissing it.

She blushed. "Why thank you, Will…"

"You're welcome," he said, batting his eyes at her. "We know that you take forever to look presentable. I wouldn't want you to hold up the show."

"Bye now," Rudolf said, turning at once and putting his back to the pair.

Sherlock and Paris waved politely as they left, but both were glad when they were gone.

"That was totally uncomfortable," Faraday said, poking his head out of the pocket.

Paris was so grateful that the actors were gone that she didn't shove him back into the compartment. "Yeah, that guy is a real egotistical jerk. And that woman needs to get a clue and spine."

The squirrel stretched. "No, I quite literally meant that being squeezed into that pocket was uncomfortable. Speaking of spines, I think I need some chiropractics after this. Can you get bigger jacket pockets?"

"Actually, speaking of deep pockets," Rudolf said in a hush, looking over his shoulder and then back to the group. "Don't look now, but the wealthiest man in the theater is making his way over here."

"Wealthiest?" Paris questioned.

"Well, besides me, of course," King Rudolf stated. "I could buy and sell him a hundred times over. But still, try not to embarrass me and I'll introduce you."

Paris gave Sherlock a dry expression. "Isn't it cute when he tells us not to embarrass him?"

"It's adorable," the great detective said, zero inflection in his voice.

Rudolf waved them off, trying to quiet them down. "Pipe down, you lot. Adults are about to be speaking."

CHAPTER THREE

Scene Three *– Lobby Bar, Agatha Theater, London, United Kingdom*

"Who let you in here?" King Rudolf cheered, striding over and shaking a man's hand with both of his. The guy was old, in the way that he was gray and wrinkled. The king of the fae was much older, but didn't look a day over forty, even if he was several hundreds of years old.

The man with a round belly and a head of gray hair chuckled. "I'd ask the same of you, if I didn't know that most would pay you to sit in one of their playhouses, King Rudolf."

The fae nodded. "But I bought these tickets for my friends and myself." He held out an arm to Paris and Sherlock in a presenting manner. "Please come and bestow your acquaintance on my guests. It's not a theater experience unless one has met the great Phillip O'Hara."

"Oh, I forgot how charming you are, King Rudolf," Phillip said, striding over.

Paris leaned into Sherlock, whispering. "I didn't. And who are these cartoon characters? Why do I feel like the acting has already started before the curtain is up?"

Sherlock nodded minutely. "I'm getting the same impression. Just pay attention and take note of everything."

Paris sighed, realizing that she would never get an actual night off for as long as she lived—which according to prophecies was going to be a long time. She sighed, noticing that large British man wore a nicer suit than William Evermore, but there was something unkept about his appearance. His undershirt was strangely wrinkled, like he'd put it on before he was dry from sitting in a sauna or something.

"May I present Paris Beaufont and Sherlock Holmes," King Rudolf said, holding out an arm to them.

"You may and you have," the large man said, smiling wide, but the gesture not reaching up to his eyes. "Pleased to meet you, both. Phillip O'Hara. Pleasure making your acquaintance."

As the man with fat fingers wrung her hand and then Sherlock's, Paris got the impression that he couldn't repeat their names because he hadn't heard it. She was a Beaufont and sometimes recognized. But Sherlock Holmes was always noticed since most thought he was a fictional character.

Phillip's attention appeared to be darting between the pair in front of him and around the lobby to the many other play-goers filing into the space.

"Tell me, my boy," Rudolf began causally, taking hold of his third martini. "What's tonight's play about? I hadn't had a chance to check the marquee."

"What's that?" Phillip asked, pulling his focus from the concession area where the queue was quite long.

"The play," Paris offered, wondering if the fat man was hankering for a snack, based on the eager look on his face.

"Oh, who cares," Phillip said, waving her off. "It's going to be total rubbish. Everything that comes out of Agatha Theater is lousy."

"Then why are you here?" Sherlock asked, narrowing his eyes at the man.

"For the actors, of course," Phillip said and strode for the concession area, not bothering to say any goodbyes.

"Lovely man," Rudolf said, turning to face Paris and Sherlock. "I mean, he smells like he ran a marathon, but who am I to fault him for trying to get into shape."

"Very curious actually," Faraday said, having poked his head up again out of the pocket.

Paris decided to allow it. "He wasn't lovely at all," she said to her uncle. "He was rude and dismissive. And why does he come to Agatha Theater if he doesn't like their offerings?"

"Oh that," Rudolf said, nodding. "Well, you see, Phillip owns many of the playhouses here in the West End. He's been trying to get the owner of Agatha Theater to sell to him or make him a partner, but she isn't interested. So he shows up nightly to put the pressure on her. Rumor has it that the critics that give the plays here bad reviews have their pockets padded by Phillip."

Paris huffed, offended. "That's horrible."

"It is, but it's not a crime." It was Sherlock Holmes who interjected this, his calculating gaze following Phillip O'Hara as he bought something at the concession area, sliding his credit card across the counter and seeming impatient as he waited for it to be returned.

"No, but it's still really immoral," Paris argued. "How is this place supposed to remain in business if it's constantly fighting bad reviews and then also having to sink money into repairs?" She pulled her gaze up to the elaborately painted ceiling that also looked badly in need of repair.

"You have such a heart, Paris," Rudolf stated, patting her shoulder affectionately. "And all this place needs to stay in business is a big name on the marquee. Unfortunately, that's William Evermore. He may be a total tool, but the audiences usually adore him. It's no wonder he lands every big role here, although there are certain people who would definitely kill for it."

Paris was about to ask what Rudolf meant, but it was actually

Sherlock Holmes that broke away from the group, waving for them to follow.

"Where are you going?" she asked him.

"To concessions," the detective said, striding for the snack area, although his eyes were following Phillip O'Hara who was briskly striding away, nothing in his hands.

"Oh, good," Rudolf exclaimed. "I could use some popcorn to soak up those martinis. Then more martinis to soak up all the drama. Then repeat."

CHAPTER FOUR

Scene Four – *Concessions, Agatha Theater, London, United Kingdom*

"What can I get for you?" a small, young woman asked when they got to the front of the concession stand.

Sherlock Holmes leaned forward, inspecting the offerings, like trying to decide what treats could satisfy his hankering.

"Do you have nachos?" King Rudolf asked the woman.

She shook her head, her long brown ponytail waving back and forth.

Rudolf snapped his fingers through the air. "Sorry, Pare. Can I buy you some Twizzlers instead?"

"I'm good," Paris said. She decided to take a page out of Sherlock's book, who seemed to be covertly investigating. She offered the woman behind the counter a polite smile. "What do you recommend?"

"I'm a fan the chocolate covered peanuts," she answered, a small smile lighting up her brown eyes but quickly fading. "But sadly, we're not offering those anymore. I can sell you some candy or popcorn.

"Why aren't you selling peanuts anymore?" Sherlock asked, tilting his head to the side with curiosity.

The young woman cut her eyes to the main door that led to the auditorium. "Mr. Evermore…"

Rudolf nodded, understandingly. "He has a peanut allergy. I understand that. One sneeze and he'd be dead."

The woman's eyes widened suddenly. "No, it's nothing like that. It's that he says that constant chomping by guests is distracting to his ability to focus." There was an obvious frustration boiling beneath the surface in the mousey woman's demeanor. "I know real actors that it wouldn't bother."

"Are you a real actress, Miss…?" King Rudolf asked and although the question sounded rude, it wasn't coming from him.

"Miss Violet Clementine," she answered, blushing at the fae as many women did. Not Paris or any Beaufont woman, but other females were struck by his charm since they didn't know him well enough. "And no. I have no interests in the stage. But there are many fine actors who could easily fill the lead roles here at Agatha Theater and I'd love to see them try. They definitely wouldn't lose focus from patron chewing on snacks."

Sherlock nodded. "Good actors don't lose focus. Now may I get a pack of gum, please?" Paris was surprised when the man pulled out a credit card. She didn't think he used any modern things or pay with anything but shillings or whatever.

Violet apparently was surprised too. "Oh, we actually don't take credit cards." She pointed to a sign that said, "Cash Only."

Sherlock nodded. "Of course. I must have missed that."

Paris narrowed her eyes in speculation at the great detective. She very much doubted that he missed anything at all. Sherlock Holmes had seen something, and he was already investigating, even if there wasn't a crime. Paris was about to do her own inspection, but King Rudolf threaded his arm around hers and tugged her away.

"Oh, I have someone you should meet," he said loudly, for all to hear. Then he leaned in close and whispered into her ear. "She's absolutely a tight ass and totally repugnant but smile and play nice."

CHAPTER FIVE

***Scene Five** – Lobby, Agatha Theater, London, United Kingdom*

King Rudolf led Paris and Sherlock over to a woman standing all on her own. She was older, in her mid-sixties and dressed much more conservatively in a pant suit than most of the other females wearing evening gowns.

"If you came to make me an offer, King Rudolf, then you're wasting your time," the woman said in a refined British accent, no pleasantries as she pursed her wrinkled lips at the fae. Her long gray hair was pulled up in a French twist, completing the "no nonsense" look she had going.

"Oh, what bee do you have in your bonnet this time?" Rudolf asked, extending a hand to her. "Is it because you're aging so poorly or another husband has left you or just because you're a sour old bag?"

Paris kept her surprised expression at bay but still cut her eyes to Sherlock. Didn't Rudolf ask them to behave? And here he was insulting a woman who exuded a bit of power and prestige.

Sherlock's expression didn't give anything away either though as he studied the woman.

She studied the pair behind Rudolf and then the fae himself before shaking her head, dismissively. "So, you're not here to try and buy my theater."

"No, Agatha, I don't want your crumbling piece of rubble," Rudolf said, sounding rather bored. "Just a fun time with friends."

The woman continued to study him. "So you're just here to get drunk, per usual and heckle in the audience?"

He nodded. "Is that okay, Agatha?"

She seemed to consider this and then nodded, softening a bit with a slight smile. "And you know that my name isn't Agatha." The woman angled around Rudolf and extended a hand to Paris. "I'm Collette Billings, the owner of Agatha Theater and director of all its plays."

"Pleasure to meet you," Paris said, wringing her hand. "It's a beautiful theater."

"No, it's not anymore," the woman said, nodding at Sherlock but not offering her his hand. "The roof is caving in, and the plumbing all wrecked, and I swear if Phillip O'Hara isn't some-where planting termites in the walls."

"So you were worried that Rudolf was going to try to buy you out," Sherlock speculated. "Sounds like that might be wise to think about selling."

Collette shot him an annoyed look. "Would you sell your soul if it were crumbling to the ground?"

"Well, no," Sherlock answered at once.

The woman nodded proudly, looking around the lobby. "Agatha Theater might have seen better days, but it's still a wonderful place for the arts. I just need a big win. A big show that brings in a full house, night after night. The problem is, well, that I end up giving away half the tickets just to make the place not look so sad. Reputation is everything and we're failing."

"You said that Phillip O'Hara was out to get you," Paris remarked. "Why would he do that?"

"So he can buy the theater," Collette answered. "He knows I'm months away from bankruptcy. But as long as I've got William Evermore, well, then I think we'll keep the doors open. The ones who do buy tickets regularly, come to see him. I just need something else to get the rest in the door."

"It sounds like your reputation has been tarnished," Paris observed, thinking of the comment about how the critics had been bought.

Collette actually shrugged. "That's part of this game. I'm just not as good at playing it as some of the others in the West End. But my grandfather gave me this place and I'm not letting it go."

"What about offering something different than murder mysteries?" Sherlock asked. "That's a very specific genre that serves a very narrow audience."

Collette shook her head. "Oh, no. I love murder. It's my passion."

"She said that out loud," Rudolf said in a mock whisper. "Put that on your notepad that she likes to murder. If someone dies tonight, then it was definitely Collette."

"No, you imbecile," Collette spat at the king, obviously not as taken with him as the others they'd met that night. "I love mystery and following clues and bringing the audience into the midst of it all. I'm not selling out like all those others in the West End, putting on frilly musicals and things that are children friendly. My mother loved mystery and my grandfather this theater. I plan to keep both their memories alive, even if it kills me."

The lights flashed off and then back on several times on the heels of her words, making them seem extra ominous.

"Well, on that note," Rudolf sang. "I think we better take our seats since that means the show's starting. We will simply leave you to plan your funeral, Collette."

"Good," the woman said as they lined up for the door to the

auditorium. "Don't come to my funeral. I don't want you there, King Rudolf."

"Noted," he said, waving jovially, like they'd had a pleasure exchange.

CHAPTER SIX

Scene Six – *Auditorium, Agatha Theater, London, United Kingdom*

As they neared the doors of the auditorium, King Rudolf began patting his tuxedo jacket nervously, like he lost something.

"What's wrong?" Paris asked him dryly.

"I've seemed to have misplaced the tickets," he said, feeling into the inside of this jacket breast pocket.

She sighed. "Did you even get them, or did you just dream that you did?"

"I bought us boxed seats with a wonderful view of the stage and the theater itself," he said, distracted by his searching. "Just stall for a moment while I locate them. I don't want to lose our place in line."

Paris glanced over her shoulder where the queue was rather long. She shared an annoyed look with Sherlock Holmes. "Ready to make small talk with the usher?"

"Actually, yes," the detective said, striding up to the man in the usher's uniform. "I have a few trigger issues and was wondering about this play and if could have any affects on my PTSD."

"Oh, you should be fine," the man answered in a cockney accent. He was somewhat plain and lanky and good natured with a wide smile. "I mean, if murder is okay. *What's Buried in the Garden* is a brilliantly fun play but chock full of death."

"Did you say, '*What's Buried in the Garden?*'" Paris asked. "That's the name of the play?"

The man nodded, excitedly. "Oh, yes. It's a melodrama about a dysfunctional family who accidentally are a part of a murder and after that, well, everything goes badly. Murder after murder after murder."

"Are you at all concerned that you've told us too much about the plot?" Sherlock Holmes asked the guy.

He chuckled, covering his mouth. "I'm sorry. Darn it, Charles, you did it again."

"Do you often ruin the plot of a play you take tickets for?" Paris asked, glancing at Rudolf who was still searching for the tickets.

"Just this one," the guy answered. "I just love it so much. And the one before it too. Oh, and the play that was on at the beginning of the year. They are all good."

"Do you enjoy them because you watch them every night?" Sherlock asked, that look in his eyes when he was piecing things together.

"I love it because I'm an actor," they guy who was apparently named Charles said. "I just love the stage. But I love the plays here at Agatha Theater."

"Then why don't you audition, Mr.…?" Rudolf asked, having pulled the tickets from a pocket that Paris was pretty sure he already checked.

"Mr. Charles Kingman," the man replied. "And I audition every time. But I'm no William Evermore. And that's alright. One day, I'll be up on that stage. I know my time in the spotlight is coming. But until then, I'll take tickets with a smile." Charles held out his hand to Rudolf who gave him three tickets.

"I hope that you get your part," Paris said as they continued into the theater, waving to the usher.

"Thank you, Madam," Charles Kingman sang. "Me too. And hopefully sooner, rather than later."

ACT TWO: THE PLAY

CHAPTER SEVEN

Scene One – *Balcony Box, Auditorium, Agatha Theater, London, United Kingdom*

"Who names these people?" Paris asked, looking around the theater from their balcony and watching patrons take their seats.

"I don't see what's so wrong with the character's names in *What's Buried in the Garden?*" Rudolf said, studying the program for the play.

Paris shook her head. "No, I meant the characters we met tonight. I mean, it's like they were names by a random name generator."

Sherlock nodded. "They all do have names that are rather mouthfuls."

"William Evermore and Monica Stagecoach," Rudolf said, reading from the program.

"And Phillip O'Hara and Collette Billings," Faraday said from his seat, having slipped out of Paris' coat with an exasperated sigh upon finding their seats. "They obviously loathe each other."

"And that concessions woman totally has it out for William," Paris stated. "What was her name again?"

"Apparently she's Violet Clementine," Rudolf said, pointing to the program. "She's listed here as working concessions and as a stagehand, but in the tiniest of writing. Her name is just under that nice usher's name, Charles Kingman. He seemed like a passionate fellow."

"He seemed like he'd kill for a chance to act on stage," Faraday stated tersely as the lights lowered and the curtain went up.

Sherlock tilted his head to the side, giving the squirrel a cautious look. "Remember, it's who you least suspect but who has the greatest opportunity, means and motive."

CHAPTER EIGHT

Scene Two – *Balcony Box, Auditorium, Agatha Theater, London, United Kingdom*

The curtain to *What's Buried in the Garden* opened to reveal an elegantly appointed living room with a couch in the center of the stage, a front door on stage right and stairs leading up on stage left as well as a kitchen door. Paris sat back in her seat, trying to think back to when she'd been able to relax and simply watch something for enjoyment.

She was instantly intrigued when William Evermore rushed in from the door and onto the apron of the stage, appearing frantic, his hands covered in dirt. He looked around at the audience, like he was about to ask one of them for help to his apparent problem.

"What have I done?" he asked, his voice grief stricken. "How could I have let this go this far?"

"Darling?" a woman's voice said from the wings to the left.

He jerked his head in that direction, his eyes wide with shock. "Noooo," he cried in a whisper.

"Please tell me when the gardener gets here," the woman

continued. "I want to ask him to lay off my petunias. He's totally killing them…"

William Evermore thrust his dirt covered hands into his hair, not seeming to care that he was covering himself in soil. "I told him. And it won't be happening again…ever again." He cradled his head for a moment, crying softly. Then he looked up, like he had an idea. "The petunias! Yes, no one will think to check under the prize-winning petunias."

William Evermore's character ran for the front door, opening it with his dirt covered hands and disappearing. Just then, Monica Stagecoach trotted down the stairs, humming delightedly. Her eyes darted to the dirt that had been scattered around by her husband. She growled.

"Oh, that stupid gardener," she complained. "He's tracked dirt through the house. I swear, I'll murder that man who tries my patience at every turn."

Although the play was already intriguing, Paris found her attention distracted by a small flashlight bobbing around in the audience. She narrowed her eyes at the dark area, trying to determine the cause.

There were several people sliding past one another, like there was some confusion on seats in the audience. She made out the tall figure of Charles, the usher, directing people to where to sit. He seemed flustered by the confusion, but after a moment, got everyone into place before taking a position next to the wall closest to the exit.

William Evermore's character had returned to the stage to confront his wife about what he'd done.

"The gardener!" Monica exclaimed. "How could this happen?"

"Things just got out of hand," William explained. "We started to argue and I was showing him how to shovel and he made a comment and I just swung the tool at him. I swear, darling, I never meant this to happen. I'm not a murderer."

Monica rushed at him, throwing her arms rather greedily

around William. "Of course you aren't, darling. We will fix this. We just have to cover our tracks."

Just then the doorbell rang.

Paris was quite literally on the edge of her seat, wondering what would happen next when another commotion in the audience caught her attention. She squinted in that direction. This time, she wasn't at all surprised to find Collette Billings and Phillip O'Hara arguing close to the stage. It seemed like the worse place and time to be having an argument. And by the way the actors paused, she realized that they had been distracted too.

King Rudolf rubbed his hands together, leaning forward. "And now the real drama starts."

CHAPTER NINE

Scene Three – *Balcony Box, Auditorium, Agatha Theater, London, United Kingdom*

On the house right side of the stage, opposite of Paris' balcony box, Collette and Phillip were adamantly whispering. They couldn't be heard, but their animated nature made it so that it was obvious to everyone that something was going on.

The small woman, half the size of Phillip, pushed him several feet toward the closest exit. He threw up his hands, objecting.

The actors stalled in their dialogue, definitely distracted.

"What's going on?" Paris whispered, looking sideways at Sherlock.

"Phillip was standing to the side when Collette came over to him and her lips said, 'Sit down or I'll throw you out,'" the detective explained in a whisper.

"Oh, do you think he's trying to ruin the performance?" Paris asked.

Sherlock shook his head. "I think he's trying to get under her skin so that she ruins her own play."

That made a lot more sense to Paris. Thankfully, Collette seemed to figure this out too and stomped off down the side aisle and disappeared out one of the exits to the back.

Charles Kingman was still dutifully standing next to the wall by his exit, looking very nervous as he ran his eyes over Phillip and then the actors on the stage.

They had momentarily been thrown off by the disruption, but quickly recovered.

"The neighbor saw the whole thing," Monica's character said, pacing back and forth in front of the sofa. "What are we going to do?"

William strode over to her, his arms extended. "Don't worry, darling. I'll take care of everything. I got us into this mess. I'll get us out of it."

"How?" Monica asked shrilly.

"Well, old Mr. Tillman lives alone. I'm sure that no one will notice if he goes missing…"

Monica was a great actress. The shock covering her face immediately was quickly replaced by tears. "Oh, more death. Will it ever stop. First it was the gardener, then the maid and now Mr. Tillman…"

Paris' eyes widened. "How much of the play did we miss during that drama?"

"A lot, it would seem," Faraday answered. "But thankfully Phillip seems to have taken his seat and Collette has disappeared. And even Charles doesn't have to police anymore drama." He nodded down to the house floor where things had quieted down a lot more.

Charles was leaning against the wall and Paris smiled as he mouthed all of William's words, obviously having memorized the part. She really hoped that one day he got his chance to be on the stage for real.

She also hoped that this theater stayed open and performing

murder mystery plays for a long time to come. Strangely, she had grown quite the affinity for Agatha Theater in the short period of time. But Paris had no idea, that everything was about to shift as they entered into the third act.

CHAPTER TEN

Scene Four – *Balcony Box, Auditorium, Agatha Theater, London, United Kingdom*

For the better part of an hour, Paris hardly breathed as the drama unfolded on the stage. She had never considered herself a murder mystery fan, but now she was absolutely hooked. And the strangest part was, there didn't even seem to be a mystery to the whole thing.

The husband was always behind the murders. He was the one doing them, covering them up and hiding the bodies in the garden. The poor wife was always the one stumbling onto the treachery and having to come to terms with what her husband had done. And yet, Paris knew instinctively that she was missing something. A little twist. A clever little clue that would change everything.

But there had been more than a few distractions during the three-act play. There was the seating confusion with Charles, but he'd handled easily enough. And he'd stayed in his post the entire play.

Then there had been the little tiff with Collette and Phillip.

That one had seemed really unnecessary, but simply spoke of the animosity growing between the two. Collette hadn't resurfaced after storming off. And Phillip hadn't left his seat.

Then there had been some confusion on some props that went missing. The blunder had been obvious when after burying the last body, William's character asked his wife to bring him some wine.

"I'm *still* waiting, darling," William said, drawing out each of the words, sounding really annoyed. That was William the person and not the character, wondering why Monica was scrambling around backstage.

"I'll be there in a moment, darling," Monica called from backstage. "It appears I have to open another bottle."

"But the bottle is always open and ready," William said, stressing on every syllable.

"I understand, darling but somehow it's gone missing," Monica replied.

The audience started to whisper, sensing something wasn't right with the scene.

"Can you please just bring me anything, darling?" William asked loudly. "It can be water at this point. I simply want to cheers our good fortune and that we've gotten away with it all."

"Oh, here it is!" Monica exclaimed and moment later rushed onto the stage from a side door next to the stairs. She had a goblet of red liquid in her hands and a forced smile on her face. "Sorry, dear. You know how forgetful I am. I must have misplaced your favorite wine. But here it is."

"Why thank you," William said, seeming to slip back into his role with a sigh. "And your glass?"

"Oh, I'm much too tired for wine, darling," Monica replied. "But you enjoy, and you really deserve it after all your hard work?"

William flexed his hands, grinning. "I say, all that shoveling has really given me more than a few calluses."

"Drink up and that will help with the pain, darling."

"Of course." William took the goblet of wine and drank it all in one gulp, about the way that Rudolf downed his liquor.

William wiped his mouth with the back of his hand and sighed. "That really hit the spot." Then he began to stagger. Gag. He grabbed at his throat.

Monica backed away, her eyes wide with shock. She looked him over frantically. "What's wrong, darling?"

"I've-I've-I've been poisoned," William said and slumped back onto the couch behind him, going limp immediately.

Monica looked him over, not at all scared suddenly. She toed his lifeless body. "Oh, it does appear that you've been poisoned. And by who, I wonder?" She smiled wickedly, looking out at the audience. "I guess I shouldn't have fallen for the gardener. But he shouldn't have broken my heart. Then you, my darling wouldn't have killed him when he provoked you. And the neighbor, well, he would have known about me and the gardener, so he had to go. Oh, and the maid, well, let's just say, I knew she was your little side hustle, so I ensured she was mulch too. Now they are all together in the garden and you can join them all soon too."

The lights faded to a roar of applause. There was the twist that Paris hadn't seen coming. The wife was behind it all, master minding it all and having her husband do the brilliant work.

She was clapping excitedly when the lights came back on. Monica was taking her bows. The other actors from the play were joining her—the gardener, the neighbor, the maid. But William wasn't getting up.

They continued to bow, but still the lead in the play didn't get up.

The actors halted. They all turned to regard William still slumped on the couch. Many of them exchanged confused expressions. Monica ran over. She was speaking into William's ear. Shaking him. Calling to him. But he didn't rise, only moved limply under her shaking.

Yanking her hands off him, she backed up suddenly, nearly tripping on the furniture behind her. Shocked and with her hands by her side like they were covered in poison suddenly, she screamed, and it was the realest thing Paris had heard all evening.

"He's dead! William Evermore is really dead!"

ACT THREE: THE INTERROGATION

CHAPTER ELEVEN

Scene One – *Stage, Agatha Theater, London, United Kingdom*

"He's been poisoned." Strangely enough it was the squirrel scientist who determined the cause of William Evermore's death. Faraday stood next to the dead body still outstretched on the couch on the stage, where William had fallen when he died.

The auditorium had been cleared of guests as quickly and efficiently as possible. A list of suspects immediately provided by Sherlock Holmes, had all been sequestered to the green room backstage while the investigation took place. Although Scotland Yard would be on their way, the Captain had said he was happy to have the great Sherlock Holmes and his team on the case. Apparently, getting into the West End on a weekend at that hour was nearly impossible due to traffic and it could be several hours before the police arrived.

"The wine?" King Rudolf asked, pointing to the goblet lying on the floor with purplish red liquid coating the inside. "Wine would never dare to kill anyone. If so, I'd be dead long ago."

Using a handkerchief, Paris picked up the goblet so that she didn't compromise the crime scene with her fingerprints. She sniffed the inside of the glass. "This isn't wine. It's grape juice."

Rudolf nodded. "That's common in the theater. The light actors can't handle a full glass of wine, especially when they have back-to-back performances in a night. Usually, beer is apple juice and wine is grape. It really is such a sad waste of an opportunity to get buzzed."

"But this glass…it's hot." Paris placed it on the coffee table, close to where Faraday was stationed.

He hopped over to the table, inspecting it. "Of course, it is…" The squirrel sniffed the goblet, studying the way the remnants of the liquid moved down the glass.

"Of course, it is," Rudolf chimed triumphantly. "And that is because…well, tell Paris, Faraday. I'm not sure how to explain it in a way that she'll understand."

Faraday flicked his tail, glancing toward the door that led to stage left. "Is Sherlock back there?"

Paris nodded. "Yes, he's investigating the back area where the drink and props were kept."

"Of course," the squirrel said, directing his full attention to Paris. "The poison, I believe to be a derivative of a narcotic called adina. As you may know, in Hebrew this means delicate."

"Everyone knows that," Rudolf said smugly and then waved at Faraday. "Go on. You dumb this down and explain it much better than I could."

The squirrel shook his small head at the fae before clearing his throat to continue. "The drug, although lethal if ingested, is also is very temperamental. When synthesized, it must be done at high temperatures. It isn't stable for long at room temperature but can be transported. The caveat is that when put into usable form, such as a drink meant to poison, then it must also be in something hot like when synthesized."

"Like warmed up grape juice?" Paris questioned. "What a

strange and high maintenance poison. And wouldn't William have wondered why the juice was hot?"

"Remember that he was flustered because Monica couldn't find the wine," Faraday explained. "He had been stalling and probably was willing to drink anything that she delivered. Also, the poison, although very temperamental to make and deliver, is virtually untraceable after an hour of being ingested. Therefore, if created correct, transported in a timely manner and ingested in hot liquid, it will do the trick with no traces after a set period of time."

Paris narrowed her eyes. "And there are several suspects for this murder who would know how long it takes Scotland Yard to get here at this hour."

Sherlock Holmes nodded, striding in from stage left. "My thoughts too."

"You could hear everything we were saying?" Faraday asked, surprised that the detective chimed into the conversation like he'd been there the entire time.

"Of course," Sherlock replied. "From backstage, you can easily hear everything going on here. Conversely, what happens backstage appears to be muffled, ideally to keep things quiet for the audience."

"Did you find anything back there?" Paris asked, obviously referring to the investigation.

"Not as much as I would have liked," the detective answered. "There were no traces of the container the grape juice came from or the poison. The props area did seem more disheveled than I think it's usually kept. The gardening tools appear to have been knocked over."

"Maybe Monica tripped over them while looking for the missing wine," Paris offered.

"Maybe," Sherlock mused, not looking convinced. "Whoever killed William Evermore, planned it very carefully, with great attention to detail and a thorough knowledge of this theater and this drug, adina. The only way to determine who the murderer is will be to question all the suspects. Did you detain the list I gave you into the green room?"

Paris nodded. "Yes, and I put a spell on the room so that they couldn't talk and share information. But I don't understand the list that you gave me. Some of those people definitely couldn't have done it. I had my eyes on them during most of the show."

A glint radiated in Sherlock's eyes. "Don't allow appearances to deceive you. A murderer can be behind the curtain, so to speak. And also, on that list are suspects and also those I think that will hold the information to crack this case."

CHAPTER TWELVE

Scene Two – *Auditorium, Agatha Theater, London, United Kingdom*

William Evermore's body had been covered morbidly by a white sheet and lay exactly where it had been when he died—on the stage. Paris found it strange to interrogate the suspects and witnesses of the murder with the dead body lying close by. However, Sherlock Holmes had said this was a smart strategy that often unnerved the murderer when questioned. Furthermore, it encouraged the innocent to be forthright, being reminded to the weight of the situation.

The interrogation team, which included Paris Beaufont, Sherlock Holmes, King Rudolf and Faraday, all stood in front of the stage, peering down at their first witness. Charles Kingman sat in the front of the audience, looking up at them, tension and sadness in his eyes.

Paris watched as his nervous gaze darted to the dead body behind them every so often as Sherlock Holmes began to pace. He'd been quiet for a long moment, a strategy he often used to draw out information from a suspect and also unnerve them. No one said a word, everyone knowing that the great detective would start the investigation and inevitably close it.

"Mr. Kingman," Sherlock began, his hands pinned behind his back and his chin down. "You've worked at Agatha Theater for how long?"

"Several years, sir," Charles replied at once, flashing an uncomfortable smile.

Paris had seen the usher the entire time during the play. She had zero idea how he could have poisoned the grape juice backstage. But then she remembered what Sherlock had said about the murderer sometimes being behind the curtain, in a metaphorical sense and possibly literal one, in his instance.

"And you've ushered, is that right?" Sherlock continued his questioning.

"Yes, that's correct, sir."

Sherlock paused, withdrawing his pipe from the breast pocket of his tuxedo jacket. Paris wasn't surprised to see him with it, since he was never without it. Ironically though, the man never smoked, only chewed on the end of the worn pipe and only when detecting. "But you've wanted to be an actor for quite some time, is that correct?"

"Oh, yes," he answered, his eyes wide with sudden excitement. "My passion is the stage. It's why I wanted this job here at Agatha Theater."

"And have you auditioned for the parts here?" Sherlock questioned.

"Yes, every time there's a new play," Charles stated. "But the lead always goes to William and I'm never a good fit for the other ones."

"So, you murdered William so you could have his role!" King Rudolf exclaimed, pointing an accusatory finger at Charles.

The usher peeled back a few inches, shock written on his face. "Of course not. I would never hurt him or anyone else."

Paris covered her laugh. King Rudolf seemed to always take

on the bad cop role when he was working with Sherlock Holmes. It was really amusing to watch, but she wasn't sure that it worked the same way the fae thought it did.

"And actually, I should be taking William's part in the current play anyway," Charles continued.

"Because you murdered him and he's dead!" Rudolf yelled, pointing now at the floor very melodramatically.

Charles shook his head. "Because he's…well, he *was* going to be leaving Agatha Theater. But…well, no one knew about it. Not Monica or any of the other cast or staff. I only knew because Collette had come to me individually and apologized and then offered me the lead role in the *What's Buried in the Garden*."

"William Evermore was leaving Agatha Theater…" Sherlock said, seeming to ruminate on the idea.

Charles nodded, trying to smile, but also stay remorseful. "He had a better opportunity at another, bigger playhouse. One outside London, but he didn't give Collette the details. Just said that he'd be done by the end of the month and need to be replaced. And she picked me."

"That's wonderful that you got the role," Paris began, remembering how the usher knew all the lines William had spoken when performing. "But why would Collette have apologized? I thought your dream was to act on the stage. Did she feel bad that you had to jump into the part last minute?"

The usher shook his head. "Oh, no. It was simple payroll issue. You see, William, before he found a better gig, demanded higher pay." He leaned forward, like afraid he might be overhead. "I don't know if you realize, but this place is going bankrupt." Charles said the last part in a paranoid hush, looking around nervously.

"We heard," Rudolf stated matter-of-factly.

"Well, in order to pay the salary William was demanded, Collette had to dock all the front of house's pay," Charles continued. "I didn't mind so much, because I knew if I worked hard, that my time on the stage would come and that's what I really wanted. But there were others were quite cross about it."

"Like who?" Sherlock questioned. "And did they know that it was because William wanted more money?"

Charles nodded. "There are no secrets in this theater, even when we try to be discreet. It was Violet who told me that she'd overheard William telling Collette he wanted more money. She was backstage, stocking the props when they talked. And he said that the Agatha Theater wouldn't remain open without him and that he deserved more money."

Paris cut her eyes to Sherlock, remembering what he'd just told her about being able to hear everything from backstage and realizing that this was probably all true.

"But then, Collette cried," Charles went on, "and said the only way she could afford to pay William more was to pay us, the ushers and concessions, less. Well, he was alright with that, so we all got cuts. Violet was upset, but that's understandable. That's her livelihood and she does it to survive, unlike me, who is doing it to get to a better place in my career."

Paris shook her head. "But then that double-crossing weasel took the higher salary to probably go and negotiate a better contract with a different playhouse."

She knew William had just died and she shouldn't be so harsh about him. But now that Paris was learning about his true character, she couldn't help but be angry. She reasoned he had been killed because he wasn't liked. And it was their job to find out why and it appeared that there were probably more than a few people who wanted William Evermore dead.

Sherlock nodded. "So he made an enemy out of Collette to her employees and then still was planning on leaving her high and dry."

"I have a question," Faraday began, flicking his tail.

"I'm sorry," Charles said, pointing to the squirrel. "Is the animal talking?"

"He does that," Paris answered. "But we allow it because he's usually the smartest person in the room, although not really a person."

Charles nodded, like this was a sufficient explanation. "Your question."

"You had a seating disruption at the beginning of this show," Faraday stated. "Can you tell us what the problem was?"

"Oh, nothing major." Charles waved his hand through the air dismissively. "Phillip O'Hara had sat in someone's seat and needed to be moved. But then he didn't like where he was and made quite the commotion with Collette as you probably saw from your balcony box."

Paris nodded. "That we did."

Charles shrugged. "Well, I didn't really get the whole thing. Firstly, he's at regular performances and should know the theater seats and set up well enough. And also, where I sat him is one of his usual seats, but he didn't quite like it on this occasion."

"Very curious," Faraday said, cutting his gaze to Paris, a meaningful expression in his brown eyes. They both knew that this piece of information was important, but not why.

CHAPTER THIRTEEN

***Scene Three** – Auditorium, Agatha Theater, London, United Kingdom*

The wailing sobs from Monica Stagecoach filled the large theater, taking over the space for a long minute.

Finally Sherlock Holmes stepped up, straight in front of the woman seated in the front row and looked down at her with authority.

"How did you know the deceased?"

Monica's eyes widened as she covered her face with a wet handkerchief. "Are you serious? You saw us tonight. We were costars in the play."

"But were you romantic?"

The woman's eyes darted to the body covered with the sheet on the stage and she moaned softly, letting out a small cry. She seemed to be deliberating on the question and finally shook her head. "No, William and I weren't really together. I adored him. And maybe at times, he liked me. But his career was taking off and I don't think I was as appealing to him as he was to me."

"So you killed him, didn't you?" Rudolf exclaimed, pointing an accusatory finger at the woman.

Paris wanted to slap her uncle, but also laugh at his foolishness.

"No!" Monica yelled in a hoarse cry. "But I'd kill whoever did this!"

Suddenly Paris sunk back, grateful that Rudolf had played his part. They were seeing a different part of Monica now. One that apparently wanted revenge.

"Do you know who would have killed William?" Sherlock asked, point blank.

"I don't know," Monica replied. "I'd never harm him though. But I'd really go after whoever did this. He was such a loving...well, thoughtful...well, no, but he was handsome and charming, at least. And many adored him, the same as me. I just don't understand why someone would hurt him."

"Were you aware that William was leaving Agatha Theater for another position somewhere else?" Faraday questioned.

The look of shock covering Monica's red face said that she didn't know this. "He was what? Are you certain?"

Sherlock shook his head. "No, it's speculation at this point." He gave Faraday a punishing look, like he didn't want this information released.

Paris decided to move things on to more pertinent details. "The juice that killed William, you served to him. From the audience's vantage point, you were delayed in bringing it. Tell us what happened?"

Monica sucked in a breath, perking up slightly. "Oh, it was very strange. The goblet with grape juice is always in the same spot on the prop shelf. But when I went back there to fetch it..." She motioned to the backstage area. "Well, it wasn't in its spot. So I started scrambling around, looking for the container that the juice is poured from or anything to replace it. William was really upset from the stage and I knew I was running out of option. So I ran using the crossover to the other side of the stage to try and find something, anything for him to drink. It was very stressful.

There was nothing there. So I ran back, thinking I'd get something from my dressing area, but when I returned, the goblet was in place, like I'd simply missed it all along."

"And whose job is it to stock the props and put the grape juice in the goblet in place for the scene?" Faraday asked.

Thankfully Monica didn't seem to mind having a squirrel asking her questions. Some were better with magical things in this world than others, depending on exposure. "Oh, that's Violet Clementine's job. She works concessions before the show and during intermission. But her job is to make sure that the shovel and tea and goblet and whatnot are all in place and ready for each show."

"Violet," Sherlock said, really enunciating the name. "And what was her relationship to William?"

"She didn't care for him the same as some of us," Monica stated. "She wanted Charles to have that lead role. Everyone knows that Violet is in love with him. But he doesn't care because all Charles loves is the stage and the idea of acting. Everyone knows that."

"No," Sherlock said mostly in a hush, turning to look at his team of investigators. "Not everyone knew that..."

CHAPTER FOURTEEN

Scene Four – *Auditorium, Agatha Theater, London, United Kingdom*

The longest bit of tense silence passed as Sherlock Holmes stood to the side, appraising Phillip O'Hara. His calculating gaze ran over the man's suit and wrinkled undershirt. The disheveled look to his gray thinning hair became apparent when he threw his hands through it several times. It must be a nervous habit and Sherlock was excellent at making people tense.

Phillip kept readjusting his position, crossing one leg over the other and then changing. It was then that Paris spotted the dirt on the tops of his loafers. She wouldn't have noticed it, but the dirt was fresh and sprinkled on his white socks that contrasted against his black suit pants.

She glanced down at her own shoes, spotting mud from the streets and remembering how dirty the London streets could be.

"How much longer are you going to keep us?" Phillip asked, readjusting again, his eyes glancing at his shoes. "I do have places to be."

"As long as it takes to find the murderer," Sherlock replied calmly. "Now tonight Collette mentioned that you've been doing things to run her out of business. Is that true?"

Phillip scoffed at him. "Like I care about this two-bit theater."

"Then why do you come here so often?" Paris questioned. "You said it was for the actors. Were you interested in William Evermore?"

"Hardly," Phillip answered. "I've seen better acting at my granddaughter's nursery school. But I always like to keep an eye out for talent. I'm sure that Collette is paranoid enough to think I'd steal her actors though."

"Were you aware that William was leaving Agatha Theater?" Paris asked.

Phillip shook his head, his face going white suddenly. "Wow, I bet was quite the blow to Collette. She needed him to keep her doors to Agatha Theater open."

"You and Collette were arguing tonight," Sherlock stated matter-of-factly. "Why was that?"

Phillip laughed, humorlessly. "I didn't like my seat and preferred to stand. But she wasn't having it. And made a ruckus over something that didn't need to be one. She's always blowing things out of proportion."

"But you often sit in that seat," Rudolf said, sounding strangely professional and not making wild accusations. "Why tonight was it not to your liking?"

The fat man shrugged. "I don't know. I just didn't like it. Maybe the woman next to me was wearing too much perfume or the man on the side was hogging the arm rest."

"Well, which is it?" Sherlock questioned.

"Both," Phillip decided at once. "So I was going to stand, but Collette decided to make a deal of it."

Faraday flicked his tail, narrowing his eyes at the man. "As a theater owner, I think you know that people aren't allowed to simply stand during a show because they don't like their seat."

"As a man of the arts and one of great esteem," Phillip began,

"I know that I don't have conversations with squirrels. If you all will excuse me, I have to go to the restroom and relieve myself."

"Of course," Sherlock said, standing back and waving Phillip forward. "But one last thing. At the concessions tonight, did you buy mint or strawberry gum?"

"Mint," Phillip asked.

"And you paid with a credit card, is that right?"

Phillip sighed, shaking his head. "Yes. But I really must go now. I hope you catch who did this. The West End can't use this kind of press and I hate to think what it will do to Agatha Theater's reputation."

Paris was pretty certain that Phillip didn't care what happened to Agatha Theater's reputation. She also didn't think that Phillip needed to relieve himself as he was pretending, but rather, off to do something else…

CHAPTER FIFTEEN

Scene Five – *Auditorium, Agatha Theater, London, United Kingdom*

"Where were you tonight?" Sherlock Holmes asked Collette Billings, not wasting anytime when she was seated.

She scrunched up her brow, confused. "What do you mean? I was here."

"No," Sherlock stated. "When you left during the performance. Where did you go?"

"Oh, well, I was livid," she said, her mouth forming a hard line for a moment. "That man was trying to fluster me. Phillip stood during a performance, even though he knows that's against fire brigade safety protocol. It's very strict in the theater and could get me in trouble."

"Do you think that's why he did it?" Paris asked.

Collette shook her head of gray hair, which was slightly more frizzy than earlier like she'd been outside. "No, I think he's just a jerk who tries to rile me up at every turn. He was probably hoping that I'd ruin my own show." She slumped slightly. "I'm afraid I almost did. But then poor William…"

"He was leaving Agatha Theater though," Faraday stated.

"True," Collette affirmed. "And I was sad to see him go, but I couldn't stop him. I'd done everything to try."

"Like dock the wages of the front of house to pad his salary," Rudolf stated.

"Well, yeah…" Collette looked both surprised and ashamed by the fact that they knew this.

"So when he still jumped ship you killed him out of spite!" Rudolf accused, pointing a finger at the woman.

Unflustered, she tilted her head to the side. "Of course I didn't. I was livid at William for what he did. But I've been this business all my life. You do what's right for you. That's why I took the front of house's wages to pay my star actor. It benefited me. I knew some of them were mad, but what could I do. If I had to shut my doors, then they'd have no money, not less."

"You didn't answer the question about where you went after you stormed out of the theater," Sherlock stated. "Where did you go after your tiff with Phillip O'Hara?"

"Well, I ran out to the lobby, thinking I'd get a drink," Collette answered at once. "But then, like adding insult to injury, the whole concession area was in total shambles. I wanted an espresso. But the equipment for heating up milk and making an espresso was all missing. It didn't make any sense. I really started to doubt my ability to manage a staff at that point. So I decided to simply take a walk, even though it was misting a bit. I figured that the cool air would calm me down."

Paris studied the woman, realizing that she was telling the truth. Her appearance spoke of it. She'd been out in the night air. But the important admission was about the concession area.

Paris glanced at Sherlock who was looking sideways at her with a knowing expression. She believed by the look in his eyes that he knew who the murderer was. She did too—but something was absolutely still out of place.

Like the play she'd watched that night, she was waiting for the twist. For the something, she hadn't seen coming yet.

"That's all the questions that we have for now," Sherlock stated plainly. "Will you please send Violet Clementine in here on your way back into the greenroom. Please tell the others that it won't be much longer."

"I will," Collette replied. "But I don't think Violet was in there the last little bit. She got up to go to the bathroom a while ago and hadn't returned."

The scream that cut through the air was right on cue. Everyone bolted in the direction of where it came from, directly behind them—backstage.

CHAPTER SIXTEEN

Scene Six – *Backstage, Agatha Theater, London, United Kingdom*

"I just found her like this!" Monica Stagecoach exclaimed, motioning to the body lying at her feet. It was Violet Clementine, sprawled out, her face to the side, her head badly smashed. Beside her was a prop—the dirty shovel used in that night's play to fictionally kill people. It appeared to have actually done so.

Sherlock Holmes dove down, checking the still woman. He glance up at Paris, Rudolf and Collette. "She's dead."

"I didn't do it!" Monica yelled, her voice irate. "I promise. I had just come out here to grab a jacket from wardrobe since its freezing in the greenroom and she was here."

"Of course, you didn't," Charles said, striding forward and putting a comforting arm around her shoulder.

Phillip O'Hara stood in the shadows, shaking his head, giving the usher a skeptical expression.

"She's been dead a little while," Faraday said, looking up from the body.

"Like how long?" Sherlock asked.

"Like since the questioning began, I'm guessing," Faraday

replied, looking up at Collette. "When did she go to the bathroom?"

"Oh, as soon as you put us in the greenroom," she answered. "When Charles was told to out for questioning. They strode out together."

Monica jumped out of the usher's arm, horror written on her face. "It was you! You killed her! Why? Are you a serial killer? Did you kill William too?"

"It wasn't me," Charles said in a hush. "I didn't kill William. But I heard you threaten to kill whoever did in the greenroom. Did you murder Violet, thinking it was her?"

Monica shook her head erratically. "Of course not! And everyone knows that it was Collette who killed William. She's the one who had access to all the props and backstage areas and whatnot."

"You know damn well that's not true," Collette said with a hiss. "There are plenty who have access to that area if they desire. And why would I want William dead?"

"Because he was bailing on you!" Monica fired.

Collette shook her head. "That's not a reason to go to jail. It's not even a reason to get my hands dirty."

Paris observed, her eyes darting to the various characters, watching as they turned on themselves.

Sherlock Holmes rotated, facing each of the people. "I believe I know who our killer is, both of William and Violet. I ask that you all join me in the lobby, where Scotland Yard will be arriving any moment. If you don't and choose to flee, please know, that I will find you. And your fate will be so much more horrible than if the authorities simply dealt with you.

CHAPTER SEVENTEEN

Scene Seven – Lobby, Agatha Theater, London, United Kingdom

"Tonight a man was murdered on a stage, very dishonorably in front of an audience," Sherlock Holmes began, pacing in front of the six people gathered in the lobby of the theater. "It was a disgrace because in the play, he dies. And tonight, he died the way he would have fictionally. Whoever did this, knew the play, the props and the opportunity. But more importantly, they had the means and the motive to do so."

"It wasn't me!" Monica yelled. "I gave him the drink, but I only found it."

Sherlock shook his head. "No, it wasn't you."

"And it's my theater and I'm the director, but why would I kill William?" Collette cut in.

"Because he was leaving your precious, failing theater," Phillip stated smugly. "You were punishing him. If you couldn't have him, then no one would."

"That's preposterous," Collette stated.

"No, it's not," Sherlock stated matter-of-factly. "And it makes you a very likely suspect."

"Who do you think you are to accuse me!" Collette roared.

"I'm Sherlock Holmes," he said plainly. "But I'm not accusing. I'm simply pointing out that it makes you a likely suspect, which is what the real murderer wanted. It was much safer to kill a man with known enemies than someone innocent. And once it came out that he double crossed you, as they knew it would, then you would be suspect number one."

"But I didn't do it!" Collette screamed.

"No, of course you didn't," Sherlock said simply. "The person who killed William was the one who had the most to benefit from his loss. Someone who wanted his role to go elsewhere."

Sherlock turned and faced the unassuming Charles Kingman. The man went white.

"Me!" he said, pointing to himself. "I didn't kill William. I would never. And yes, I wanted his role, but I was going to get it. And I'm not a killer."

"No, you're not," Sherlock stated. "There is someone here who would benefit greatly if William died. Then Agatha Theater would fail and Collette would be forced to sell." He turned and faced Phillip O'Hara.

All eyes turned to the fat businessman. He didn't fluster though. He actually laughed.

"Me? Really? What proof do you have?" he asked. "I don't have access to the backstage area. And I think everyone knows where I was during the play. There's no question."

"That's as you wanted it to be," Sherlock stated. "You made a scene during the play, knowing that Collette would rush over and ask you to take your seat. But the bigger part of that was, that the detective in the audience watching everything would know that you weren't in a place to kill William when the death actually happened."

"That's simply ridiculous!" Phillip boomed. "I've had enough of this. I didn't kill William."

"No, you're right. You didn't," Sherlock stated, somewhat surprising the group.

"Wait, if it wasn't one of us, then who was it?" Monica asked. Then her eyes darted to the theater where Violet's body still lay. "Do you mean that it was Violet? But still, someone killed her."

"I'm guessing it was the person who found her," Phillip said flippantly.

"It wasn't me!" Monica yelled.

Sherlock began pacing again. "Yes, it was Violet who I've deduced killed William Evermore. She wanted Charles to have that role more than she wanted her own wages or her own position, because at the end of the day, she loved him. And since she didn't know that he had the role because William was leaving Agatha Theater, she didn't realize that her efforts weren't necessary."

Charles' mouth dropped open. "Violet? She killed William?"

"Yes," Sherlock stated.

"But she's dead," he said, almost crying.

"That's right," Sherlock said. "Because the real murderer, is the one who put her up to it. And then when she felt guilty and was about to come to the authorities, *he* went after her. Realizing that her conscience was about to overpower her desire for revenge and getting what she wanted, Phillip O'Hara decided to simply kill Violet Clementine."

"Oh, I refuse to listen to any more of this!" Phillip said, striding for the exit just as red lights filled the front doors as the authorities made their way to the theater.

"I'd caution you about leaving," Sherlock said, clear and loud. "If you do, then you're resisting arrest and that means, everything from this point will go worse for you."

Phillip wheeled around, throwing his hands up in the air. "You have no proof!"

"That's actually where you're wrong," Faraday said, jumping up on a high table, looking up at the man. "The substance used to kill William was adina, a drug that must be synthesized at hot temperatures. I think that most of us would suspect that you put on your undershirt when you were quite sweaty, is that right?"

"I'm a large man!" Phillip stated. "I sweat."

"But when you gave the drug to Violet to put into the grape juice," Sherlock cut in, "you did it by handing her your credit card. The drug was in a powder inside a small bag attached to the back of the credit card. She took it, pretended to run your card, but in actuality grabbed the drug to later lace into the warm grape juice. And she would never need your card, since the concessions don't take those…"

Phillip shook his head. "That's all speculation."

"And then," Paris began, pointing down to his shoes. "You went after Violet when you all were in the greenroom, believing she was about to confess. You found her in the backstage area and you both argued, but we couldn't hear it from the auditorium where we were talking to Charles. You grabbed the dirty shovel, and hit her in the head with it, covering your shoes in dirt."

He laughed at this. "But my shoes are spotless, so your accusation is unfounded."

"Lift up your pant legs," Paris ordered, narrowing her eyes at him.

"Do it!" Sherlock demanded.

"Oh, fine," Phillip stated, gathering up his trousers and lifting them enough to show his white socks, sprinkled in dirt.

Gasped sounded from around the group.

"This proves nothing!" Phillip exclaimed.

"Maybe not," Sherlock said, toggling his head back and forth. "But the fingerprints on the shovel and a search of your residence for remnants of the drug that killed William should be enough. And I dare say, the police like me enough to take my hunches when I supply them."

Just then, many police officers rushed into the theater, all charging in their direction.

"Please, take this man away," Sherlock Holmes said, pointing at Phillip O'Hara. "I'll be giving the Captain my full report, just as soon as I can."

"You can't do this!" Phillip yelled but was quickly led away.

The group was heavy and nothing felt truly resolved with the abruptness of having Phillip tugged away.

Monica was crying again. Charles seemed to have forgiven her for accusing him and put his arm around her and led her out to the exit to get fresh air.

Collette sighed heavily. "I can't believe this. It will really make this place the talk of the West End."

"Will that be good for business or bad?" Paris asked.

Collette shook her head. "Honestly, the best thing for my business is that I won't have to battle with Phillip O'Hara. I don't think I have to tell you, that we played differently. I never stooped down to his level and I always paid for it. I almost paid for it with my life tonight. I'm certain he wanted me to go down for this."

"I'm certain you're right," Rudolf said, smiling at the woman. "Why don't I take you for a drink. I think you really deserve one after all this."

"Thanks, King Rudolf," she replied. "You're not all that bad, after all. And your friends are nice and very helpful."

Rudolf smiled at Paris and Sherlock Holmes before offering his arm to Collette. "My friends are the best thing about me."

The pair strode for the door and disappeared like the others.

Paris turned to Faraday, picking him up. "I guess, you freeloader want to ride home in my coat pocket."

He nodded, smiling up at her.

"And I think that after tonight, I'm ready to return home too," Sherlock Holmes stated. "May I accompany you two? It's a crazy world out there and there is a lot of danger."

"Yes, thank you," Paris said, taking the arm he offered her.

"But will you remind me of something the next time I want to take a day off?"

"What's that?" Sherlock questioned.

"Don't," she stated, striding for the exit of Agatha Theater, arm and arm with Sherlock Holmes and her sidekick.

It had been a big night. A strange one. But they could all sleep peacefully, knowing that they'd solved a murder.

One more murder down—and many more to solve.

Thank you to all the long-term readers for picking up this collection of short stories. I hope the exclusive, bonus murder mystery (Murder at the Theater) really entertained and possibly stumped you. And if you're new to our books, well, I hope you're hooked. I write Urban Fantasy with a hint of mystery.

If you're a regular reader of mine and these aren't your first author notes to read, well you might know that I'm a bit eccentric. If you're new to me as an author and just meeting my words for the first time, buckle up. The author notes might be at the end and seem like afterthoughts, but they are the coarse rambling of my mind and usually only things my therapist should hear. Ha! I don't have a therapist, so get out your notepad, Dr. Reader and be ready to give me a full diagnosis by the end.

As those of you who know me have learned by now, I didn't have the same Cracker-Jack-poppin'-Disney-immersive-Leave-It-To-Beaver upbringing as most my age. While most young girls of the 1990s were watching the Little Mermaid and wanting a prince to whisk them off their tails (still haven't seen that movie…does she get feet?), I was watching Doctor Who and wishing a man would land in my living room in a blue box and whisk me through time and space.

Along with that untraditional education, while normal girls were reading their Nancy Drew, I was watching Masterpiece Theater on PBS with Hercule Poirot. Later I'd pick up a few retellings of Sherlock Holmes and find a new detective I treasured. Is it ever a wonder that I've fallen in love with writing murder mysteries? It's definitely not because I like murder. I can't even watch a tame horror movie. No, I love following the clues and unraveling the secrets of complex lives to figure out who had the best means, motive and opportunity.

Back to my childhood…

Adjusts pillow on the couch as I stretch out.

I grew up in the backwoods of East Texas in a neighborhood full of vacation rental houses. We were really the only "locals." I realize that makes me the country girl that the city-folk all thought spoke funny. "If you ain't got something nice to say, then get off my property before I release the dogs. Rambo hasn't eaten his breakfast yet…"

Do you see how I do that? It's effortless. Just a total derailment of the narrative and a tangent to boot. Yeehaw!

Anyway, my point is, I grew up in a neighborhood with a lot of houses that were empty most the time. Often, I'd find myself without a Masterpiece Theater to watch and a curious nature to satisfy. That's when I'd find myself hunting through the neighborhood, peeking in windows and looking for the mystery that needed solving.

I wished I could say that I caught the jewel thief, or my investigations led to the arrest of a masked murderer. My childhood wasn't that interesting. Once I found an unclassified mushroom that was sent to a lab and later named after the scientist who "found it." I'm not bitter. I just wanted my Sarah fungi. Is that so wrong?

Another time I found a dog that belonged to someone else.

My mother stole it though. A story for another time. And there was the time I found the puppy that would later die in my arms.

Oh...she told a dead puppy story.

Please don't write that down, Dr. Reader...

My point, is that I've always loved mystery. I've loved the traditional detective stories for all my life—hence the Agatha Theater in our last story here. For that particular tale, I pulled out many of my three-act plays from high school. I starred in quite a few mystery plays, one of them being All About Agatha (not the author). It was being reminded of those plays that gave me the idea for the three-act formatting of that story. Wasn't that fun!

All of these experiences have led me to love weaving together a mystery with the element of magic and urban fantasy components. It's just plain fun! And I hope you like them too because I honestly doubt this will be my last one. There are so many possibilities. Murder at the Races! Murder at the Dorm! Murder in a Bookstore! So much murder and so little time!

Okay, I think I'm done now...

So Dr. Reader, what have you decided, while I sat on the couch and expunged all the ramblings from my brain? Am I crazy? Is it curable? No... Well, then what can I do? I guess I'll hang out with others who are just as crazy as me.

And without further ado, I present to you the craziest of them all, our ringleader at LMBPN—Michael-Freaking-Anderle.

Much love and Peace,
Tiny Ninja

MICHAEL'S AUTHOR NOTES

WRITTEN OCTOBER 28, 2022

Thank you for not only reading this book but these author notes as well!

Let's talk about...murder?

I can't say I was much into murder mysteries because to me, the deed was done and the question wasn't "Will he or she live" but who killed them?

I wanted the dead person to come back to life!

Which recently happened in the news.

I just tried to find the info and failed, but I've recently seen headlines in my Apple News about an heir who had faked their death because of family fights over money.

THAT is a "coming back from murder (potentially)" solution I didn't / wouldn't have seen coming.

And I lie for a living.

Having said all that about murder mysteries, I do love a good challenge that has a bit of mystery to it. How to accomplish something for the company? I often dig deep to go figure it out. Unfortunately, a book/set of plots/artwork or whatever might sit on the side of my desk while I go gallivanting off in search of an answer.

That's…*bad*, right?

One of the biggest challenges for authors…

One of the biggest challenges authors face is the urge to do ANYTHING but write the next sentence in the book. Seriously.

The. Hardest. Thing.

Well, until you need to write the BLURB for the book, and you realize your ability to fabricate a story has no direct bearing on your ability to write the sales copy you need to provide to hopefully induce a reader to pick up your book and read it.

That sh#t is murder.

It got so bad for me one year that I joined Bookbub just to acquire enough of their sales emails to review how they created those compelling tiny paragraphs of copy over and over.

I eventually, after wanting to drink myself senseless if I had to write another blurb out of the blue, pulled out dozens of those emails. Once I had them together, I opened Excel and tore apart the structure of their copy.

From that knowledge, I created the methodology we use here at LMBPN to write our blurbs, and one of our authors built a white paper around it.

I felt rather special when Marc Stiegler shared it with others in the company.

That my method had intrigued a great man like Marc, a god-like explainer who takes complicated @!#% and simplifies it for my itty-bitty mind, to take his personal time to write a white paper?

I still smile every time I think about it.

So, murder is here and ~~I blame Sarah~~ I give Sarah all the credit for driving the ~~stake~~ effort to make these stories happen.

I do hope you enjoy every…last…word.

Stay warm. Talk to you soon in a future book!

Ad Aeternitatem,
Michael Anderle

MORE STORIES with Michael's newsletter HERE: https://michael.beehiiv.com/

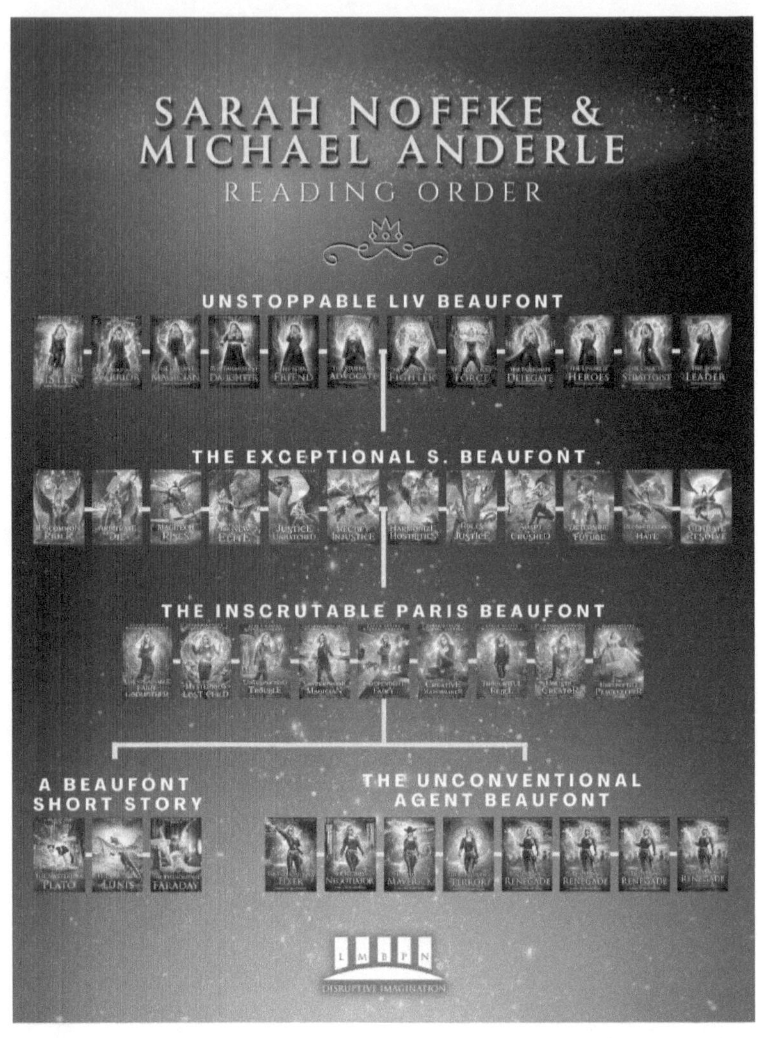

For the most up to date list please visit
https://lmbpn.com/reading-orders/sarah-noffke-and-michael-anderle-reading-order/

CONNECT WITH THE AUTHORS

Connect with Sarah and sign up for her email list here:

http://www.sarahnoffke.com/connect/

Michael Anderle Social

Website: http://lmbpn.com

Email List: http://lmbpn.com/email/

https://www.facebook.com/LMBPNPublishing

https://twitter.com/MichaelAnderle

https://www.instagram.com/lmbpn_publishing/

https://www.bookbub.com/authors/michael-anderle